CRUISES CAN BE DEADLY

SAGE GARDENS COZY MYSTERY

CINDY BELL

CONTENTS

Chapter 1	1
Chapter 2	15
Chapter 3	29
Chapter 4	43
Chapter 5	57
Chapter 6	71
Chapter 7	85
Chapter 8	101
Chapter 9	113
Chapter 10	127
Chapter 11	137
Chapter 12	147
Chapter 13	155
Chapter 14	165
Chapter 15	179
Chapter 16	193
Chapter 17	201
Chapter 18	209
Chapter 19	215
Also by Cindy Bell	225
About the Author	231

Copyright © 2020 Cindy Bell

All rights reserved.

Cover Design by Annie Moril

All rights reserved. No part of this publication may be reproduced or transmitted in any form or by any means, electronic or mechanical, including photocopy, recording, or any information storage or retrieval system, without permission in writing from the publisher.

This is a work of fiction. The characters, incidents and locations portrayed in this book and the names herein are fictitious. Any similarity to or identification with the locations, names, characters or history of any person, product or entity is entirely coincidental and unintentional.

All trademarks and brands referred to in this book are for illustrative purposes only, are the property of their respective owners and not affiliated with this publication in any way. Any trademarks are being used without permission, and the publication of the trademark is not authorized by, associated with or sponsored by the trademark owner.

ISBN: 9781658348751

CHAPTER 1

"Wow, this place is fancy." Samantha spun around in a slow circle as she looked up at the chandeliers that lined the hallway. It was a far cry from the small villa she lived in. Although she loved her home in the retirement community Sage Gardens, the luxury of the hotel made her a little giddy. "Are you sure we're in the right hotel?"

"This is it." Eddy nodded after he looked up from his phone. "I'm glad we were able to drive here. It looks like we beat the crowd." He tipped his head towards the front desk. "We'd better get ourselves checked in before the airport shuttle arrives."

"Good idea." Walt nodded as he pulled his wallet

from his pocket. "Maybe they'll let us in our rooms early."

"Look at that beauty." Jo's gaze landed on a large portrait that hung over a small bar set up adjacent to the front desk. "I could stare at it for hours."

"As long as you just stare, and don't steal." Eddy winked at her.

"Eddy!" Samantha rolled her eyes.

"It's all right, Sam." Jo crossed her arms as she stared at the painting. "I can't say that it's not a little tempting."

Once they had checked in, Walt led the way towards the elevator. Then he pushed open the door beside it, which led to the stairs.

"Walt, the elevator is right here." Samantha caught his arm.

"Oh, but the stairs are much safer." Walt glanced back at them. "Haven't you read the latest warnings about building standards in this area?"

"Uh, no." Eddy gazed at him. "I'm not hauling my suitcase up the stairs. I'm taking the elevator."

Walt shifted from one foot to the other as his friends stared at him.

"Oh yes, you're right. It would be much easier to take the elevator, and I'm sure nothing will go wrong." He took a deep breath, as Samantha held the elevator doors open for him. "All right, just a quick trip on the elevator." He nodded, then smiled at Jo as he stepped inside.

"Here we go." Jo smiled as she settled against the back wall of the elevator.

Walt wrapped his hands around the railing. He closed his eyes as the elevator rocked upward. He didn't open them again until he heard a subtle ding and the swish of the doors. Then it took him a second to get his hands dislodged from the railing.

"Walt, pal, if it's this bad in the elevator, how are you going to feel on the seven-story cruise ship?" Eddy pulled off his hat and scratched at the top of his head.

"Everything takes a little adjusting." Walt took a deep breath, then released it. "But I will adjust."

"One step at a time, Walt." Jo gave him a light pat on the shoulder. "No worries."

"Elevators get to me sometimes too, Walt." Samantha held the elevator door open so that they could all step off.

"Really?" Walt met her eyes. "You always seem so fearless, Samantha."

"Fearless?" Samantha grinned. "I'm a lot of things, but fearless is not one of them. I once got stuck in an elevator, and ever since then, I'm always a little nervous when I push the button."

"That's good news." Walt smiled as he stepped into the hallway. "Since you've already been stuck in an elevator once in your life, statistically you are far less likely to ever be stuck in one again." He raised one finger in the air. "That means that from now on, I should only take elevators with you."

"That works for me." Samantha grinned. "We can be elevator buddies."

"Whatever buddies you decide to be, make sure you're downstairs at the hotel bar by eight." Eddy paused in front of the door of his room. "I'm not missing a minute of free anything, because once we're on that ship everything is going to be extra."

"Some things are included." Samantha smiled. "My room is right next to yours." She tipped her head towards the door. "Walt and Jo, your rooms are around the corner."

"See you at eight." Jo nodded to them both then continued down the hall with Walt at her side. "How are you really doing, Walt?" She looked over at him and noted the faint twitch at the corner of his eye.

"Just fine." Walt smiled. "Well, maybe not just

fine. But I will be fine. After some rest, I'm sure I'll feel a little calmer."

"That sounds like a good idea." Jo pointed to his room. "I'm right next to you, so if you need anything just let me know."

"I've got fresh sheets and my cleaning kit, so I should be fine. But thank you, Jo." Walt unlocked the door to his room.

"I'll see you downstairs in a few hours?" Jo nodded to Walt as she moved towards her room.

"I'll be there." Walt pulled the door closed behind him.

He took a deep breath as the state of the room threatened to overwhelm him. Everything was unfamiliar, and out of place. He began to arrange things as he wanted them. He adjusted the curtains so that a good amount of light could stream in, but it would still be difficult for people to see from the outside.

"People?" He chuckled at himself. "What people, Walt? You're on the fourth floor. Maybe some birds?" He pushed the curtains wide open. His heartbeat pounded as he tried to adjust to the light that poured in. At home, he did things a certain way. But he was determined to break out of some of his habits. The wide-open curtains were a start.

After Walt changed the sheets, and cleaned the bathroom, he sat down on the edge of the bed. He selected the audio recording of affirmations that he'd been using to try to expand his tolerance of things and turned the volume up. As he stretched out on the bed, he allowed the positive messages to float through his thoughts. Soon he felt his muscles relax. He took a few deep breaths as he was instructed and pictured himself boarding the cruise ship. He'd been visualizing it for weeks. Ever since Samantha wouldn't take no for an answer about him going on the cruise of the Caribbean with his friends. Yes, they had won the vacation at a murder mystery weekend, but that didn't mean that he had to take it. According to Samantha it did.

Walt took another deep breath. A few seconds later he opened his eyes and realized that he had drifted off to sleep. The clock beside the bed indicated it was almost eight. He turned off the affirmations and stood up from the bed. As he stretched, he felt a little uneasy. He'd gone to sleep with sunlight streaming into his room, now it was dim, and still unfamiliar. He flipped on a light and hurried to get ready. Then he ducked out into the hall. When he neared the elevator, his heart began to race. He turned towards the door that led towards the stairs.

"Hey, buddy." Samantha smiled as she walked up to him. "I was waiting for you." She pressed the down button on the elevator.

"Ah, Samantha." Walt smiled. "That was kind of you."

"Don't worry, Walt, we are all here for you, whatever you need." Samantha stepped into the elevator, then offered him her hand.

"Thanks, Sam." Walt took her hand and stepped into the elevator. He knew that her gesture was out of friendship, but it still bothered him that she had to make the gesture at all. Lately, he'd had a strong desire to be normal, or at least, a little more normal. Every time he was reminded of how different he was, it annoyed him.

Samantha glanced over at him as the elevator made its way down to the ground floor. She wondered if she had pushed him too hard by insisting he join them on the trip. She could see the strain in his expression. The elevator doors slid open, and she and Walt stepped off at the entrance of the hotel restaurant.

The restaurant was filled with guests, most of them had the bright red wristbands that indicated they were part of the cruise. Samantha spotted a few open spots at the bar and headed straight for them. Although she'd done plenty of research about the cruise, she was still a little nervous about how it would go.

"Over here." She waved to Jo and Eddy, as they stepped into the restaurant. The four managed to squeeze in against the bar.

"It's crowded." Walt tugged at his collar and drew a slow breath. "I wonder what the capacity is for this space? I mean they call it a restaurant, but it's not really big enough to be considered that, is it?"

"It is tight in here." Jo leaned close to him. "We don't have to stay long."

"It's all right, I'm fine." Walt smiled.

"Free drinks will make it pretty crowded." Eddy cleared his throat. "I hope that nobody takes it too far. That's one drawback about cruises. You can't get away from people when they've had too much to drink."

"That sounds awful." Walt cringed.

"This guy looks ready to party." Samantha tipped her head towards a man who appeared to be in his late seventies or early eighties. He wore a bright blue blazer paired with a purple scarf around his neck. He leaned on a cane that appeared to be made from ivory. Despite the slight limp in his step, he moved quickly towards the bar, with a younger woman just beside him. She had a camera in her hands and pointed it right at the man.

"Would you please stand still and smile, Carson." She huffed as she adjusted the camera.

"Annabella, enough with the pictures." Carson scowled at her. He used his cane to create a space between two people at the bar. "Bartender! Drinks please!"

"We need lots of photographs. For the kids to see. Otherwise they will claim I kidnapped you." Annabella, who appeared to be in her thirties, continued to snap pictures of Carson, and the group at the bar, as she laughed.

"Yes, it looks like Carson is intent on having a good time." Eddy grinned but ducked his head to the side in an attempt to hide behind Samantha.

"Stop, it's no big deal." Samantha gave him a light shove.

"I don't want to end up plastered all over someone's social media account." Eddy rolled his eyes, then took a sip of his drink.

"It's not like you would ever see it." Samantha

smiled. "The only time you crack open a web browser is when you have no other choice."

"I'm learning." Eddy grunted.

"I've been trying to teach him." Walt shifted on the barstool. "But he gets easily distracted."

"Did you know that you can play checkers with people all over the world?" Eddy raised an eyebrow. "It has proven to be quite a challenge."

"You're addicted, aren't you?" Jo leaned over to give him a pat on the shoulder.

"I'm not addicted. I just enjoy a challenge." Eddy shrugged.

"Annabella, stop. No more pictures, please." Carson sighed and waved his hand towards the camera. "You can't enjoy life if you're always looking at a camera screen."

"Carson, can't you just let me have a few?" Annabella sighed. "Your nephews are going to want to know what you have been up to. I said I would send some photos to them."

"I'm so sorry, my love." Carson wrapped his arm around her shoulders and pulled her towards him for a passionate kiss.

Annabella pushed Carson away without too much force and glared at him.

"Carson, you know better."

"Please Annabella, no one here cares." Carson sighed, then picked up his drink.

Samantha's glass slipped out of her hand. Luckily it only dropped a few inches to the bar and landed with a small thud and a light splash.

"My love?" Samantha muttered. "I thought she was his daughter this whole time. What kind of age gap do you think that is? Fifty years?"

"Fifty might be a bit of an exaggeration." Jo picked up a napkin and wiped up the spill on the bar. "She's definitely much younger, though."

"He must be a wealthy guy." Eddy chuckled. "To get a woman like that to hang all over him."

"Eddy!" Samantha elbowed him in the side. "Is that what you'd want? Someone as young as that?" She looked over at him with wide eyes.

"Me?" Eddy shook his head. "Not a chance. Young women are too hard to keep up with." He grinned as he took a sip of his drink.

"Nice Eddy." Samantha huffed.

"Don't let him get to you, Sam, he's just teasing." Jo stood up from the barstool. "I'm pretty worn out. I think I'm going to turn in." She checked her watch. "What about you, Walt? Want to get a good night's sleep before your adventure tomorrow?"

"Uh, not just yet. I'm going to have another

drink." Walt flashed her a smile, then looked back at his glass.

"All right then." Jo turned towards Samantha. "Are you going to be okay with these two?"

"They're going to have to be all right by themselves. I'm going with you." Samantha dropped some cash on the bar for a tip, then stood up. "Good luck, boys." She eyed Eddy. "Watch out for those young women."

"I'll do my best to dodge them." Eddy smiled as he looked back at her. "Don't forget. We need to be at the dock by nine in the morning. Not a minute later or we're going to miss the boat."

"You're telling me not to forget?" Samantha shook her head. "I'm the one that set the alarm on your phone, remember?"

"Yes, yes I remember." Eddy rolled his eyes. As he took a sip of his drink, he noticed Carson and Annabella had managed to get a table. Or perhaps they bought themselves a table. Either way, they had settled, and Annabella had finally put down the camera. Eddy smiled to himself as he started to look away, but his attention was caught by the flash of another camera. He looked in the direction of the flash and saw a young man in a business suit with broad shoulders and his black hair in a ponytail. He watched as the man took another picture of Annabella and Carson, this time with the flash off. It seemed odd to him that someone would be targeting other people for photographs. Maybe he knows them? Maybe he's a reporter? Eddy frowned and turned his attention back to Walt.

"How are you holding up, Walt?"

"I'm fine." Walt shrugged, though he hadn't touched his first drink, nor had he ordered a second. "How well do you think they wash these glasses?"

"Eh, I try not to think about it." Eddy shrugged.

"Excuse me, could I have a whiskey sour?" The man who had been taking the photos pushed between Walt and Eddy to reach the bar. His crisp business suit brushed against Eddy's elbow. "Sorry." He glanced at Eddy. "It's so crowded in here, it's hard to get any service."

"It's fine." Eddy nodded. "We were just leaving. Would you like my spot?" He stood up from his barstool.

"That's kind of you." The younger man nodded as he received his drink. "Had enough already?"

"I want to be fresh for the cruise tomorrow." Eddy tipped his head towards the band on the man's wrist. "I see you're a passenger as well?"

"James Barker." He offered his hand to Eddy. "It's a pleasure to meet you."

"You as well, James. I'm Eddy Edwards, and this is my friend, Walt Right." He gestured at Walt who had stood up as well. "I'm sure we'll see you on board."

"I wouldn't count on it." James winced. "It's a working vacation for me. But thanks for the spot." He settled on the barstool.

"Excuse me." A man looked from behind thick glasses as he walked between Eddy and Walt. He sat on Walt's vacated seat beside James.

As Eddy and Walt walked away, Eddy noticed that James pulled a small camera out of his pocket. Eddy turned his attention back to Annabella and Carson at their table just as Annabella picked up a napkin and dabbed Carson's chin clean.

"Lucky fool." Eddy chuckled as he led Walt out of the bar.

CHAPTER 2

A few minutes before nine the next morning, Jo walked beside Walt, towards the giant cruise ship.

"It's so big," Walt stammered as he looked up at the ship. "It's like an entire building on water. How can that be safe?"

"Remember, we did all kinds of research on the cruise ship company's safety record. We read that article about how the size of the ship actually makes it safer?"

"I remember. I also remember reading about the few incidents where a ship got caught in ferocious storms and passengers got injured." Walt sucked in his breath. "It's rare, but it happens."

"It's very rare." Jo slipped her hand into his. "Just take a breath."

"Yes, I'll take a breath." Walt took a deep breath. He smelled the various scents that wafted off the ship. His stomach twisted as he realized that he'd be stuck breathing that for a week. All of the mixed smells, the germs from all over the world, the foods that might not be prepared properly. There would be no escaping it. He shuddered from the tips of his toes to the top of his head.

"Walt, are you okay?" Jo tightened her grasp as she felt him tremble. "Do you need a minute?" She looked towards Eddy and Samantha who had already gone up the ramp and were standing near the railing on the ship.

"Yes, a minute." Walt couldn't catch his breath as he spoke. He willed himself not to lose it in front of Jo.

"Take your time." Jo smiled at him. "Don't worry, we can do this together."

"But we're not doing it together, Jo." Walt met her eyes. "You can walk up onto that ship and be just fine. For me, it's like climbing a mountain."

"I know that, I do, Walt. I can't understand exactly how you feel, but I'll be by your side every step of the way." Jo gazed back at him. "Just like we practiced."

"Just like we practiced," Walt repeated, then looked back at the towering ship. Yes, they had practiced visualizing going up onto the ship. Jo had found audio recordings of the noises he would hear on the ship so that he could get familiar with them. She had worked so hard to try to get him to be normal. But he would never be. He had compulsions, and although he could work to ease some of them, the truth was, he would likely always have them. What was the point of trying to pretend that he could be something different, if he never could?

"I can't do it." Walt shook his head as he took a step back from the ramp of the ship and pulled his hand free of Jo's. "I'm so sorry."

"It's okay, Walt." Jo took his hand again. "We'll go up together."

"No!" Walt drew his hand away, then sighed. "Jo, I'm sorry." He met her eyes. "I really did want to be able to do this. I've been psyching myself up for it. I've been chanting affirmations. But." He looked up at the humongous ship and the people that milled around on the numerous decks. "I just can't. If I could, I would. I hope you know that."

"Of course, I do." Jo smiled at him. "It's all right, Walt."

"No, it's not all right. I wanted this to be a nice time for all of us." Walt gazed down at his polished shoes. "I wish I wasn't this way, Jo, I really do."

"Walt." Jo placed her hands gently on his shoulders and waited until he looked up at her. "You should never apologize for who you are. If this isn't a fun experience for you, then you shouldn't try to make yourself do it. Lots of people don't like to go on cruises, just like lots of people don't like to go on airplanes. It's fine. There's nothing for you to be ashamed of, got it?"

"I guess." Walt smiled some.

"I'll stay here with you." Jo picked up her suitcase and started to walk back towards the parking lot.

"No, Jo." Walt took the suitcase from her hand and handed it over to one of the stewards. "Please, make sure this gets aboard."

"Sure thing, sir." The young man offered a bright smile which revealed braces across his teeth. He carried the suitcase up the ramp.

"Walt! What are you doing? That has all of my clothes in it." Jo frowned and started after the steward.

"Jo." Walt caught her hand and pulled her back to him. "Please. I will feel terrible if I think I've ruined a fun vacation for you. If you really want me to be okay with not being able to get on that ship, then you're going to have to go and enjoy yourself." He looked into her eyes. "Do you think you can do that for me?"

"But you'll be stuck here all by yourself. Are you going to go back home?" Jo frowned.

"No, it's a few hours drive. I'll wait for you to return. I don't mind having a vacation in a nice, clean hotel room. At least, it will be clean when I'm done with it. That way we can all spend a night together after the cruise. It'll be fine." Walt gave her hand a light squeeze. "Send me lots of pictures. And we can video chat, when you're not too busy drinking those drinks with the little umbrellas." He paused, then continued. "But not too many, okay? And don't stand too close to the railing. Oh, and also be careful of the food—"

"I'll be fine." Jo laughed as she hugged him. "I'll check in with you as soon as we are at sea and I have internet access. Are you sure you're okay with this?"

"Absolutely." Walt breathed a sigh of relief as he

took another step away from the cruise ship. "Some things are just not for me."

"I understand, Walt." Jo leaned close and placed a light kiss on his cheek.

Walt's face heated up as the tickle of her lips on his skin lingered even after she walked up the ramp. Maybe she didn't really understand. But she certainly did try. She tried harder than anyone ever had in the past. That had to mean something, didn't it? He blended in with a crowd of well-wishers that were there to see the passengers off. As he waved to his friends, he didn't feel an ounce of regret. Jo was right. He wouldn't have enjoyed a minute of the cruise, and she would have been stuck reassuring him the entire time. He really could enjoy his vacation on his own in his hotel room. Still, he hoped that Jo wouldn't realize that he was just a little too different for her to tolerate. He knew in time she probably would, but would seven days on a cruise ship with all kinds of normal men speed that along?

Jo leaned close to the railing and waved both hands at Walt.

"Have fun!" She shouted to him, though he could barely hear it.

"Get back from the railing!" Walt huffed and

waved back at her. Then he laughed as her long, dark hair blew into her face, propelled by the wind off the water.

"See ya, pal!" Eddy waved to him.

Samantha held up her phone and pointed to it.

Walt's phone buzzed. He pulled it out of his pocket and found a text from Samantha.

Don't have too much fun without us!

And of course, there was a smiley face.

Walt waved to the three of them again. Maybe he couldn't get on the cruise ship, but he sure did feel lucky to have the friends that he did.

Eddy squinted at the dock as the ship pulled away.

"He'll be fine, right?" He frowned.

"He'll be much happier on shore than out here." Samantha nodded and wrapped her arm around his shoulders.

"He made me promise that we'd have a good time." Jo stepped away from the railing. "So, don't make me break my promise."

"Let's get settled in." Eddy glanced at his watch. "I say we get unpacked and then take a look around. I like to know the lay of the land."

"Land?" Jo grinned. "I think you're a little lost, Eddy."

"Ha ha." Eddy winked at her. "Meet you ladies back here at about eleven?" He raised an eyebrow.

"We'll be here." Samantha nodded.

"Let's find our cabin." Jo hooked her arm around Samantha's and tugged her across the crowded deck. "I guess Eddy will be solo now."

"Jealous?" Samantha glanced at her and smiled. "I'm sure it's going to be an adjustment for you to share a space with me."

"I'll be fine. We've shared a room before." Jo laughed. "I'm looking forward to finding out more of the little quirks that make you, you, Sam."

"There are plenty, trust me." Samantha pointed out their cabin halfway down the corridor. "That's it. It's supposed to be a luxury size, so hopefully we won't be too crammed together." She unlocked the door, and pushed it open. The sight of the space beyond made her take a sharp breath. "Where's the rest?"

"Uh, right here." Jo pointed to the tiny bathroom. "Is that toilet in the shower?"

"Okay, deep breaths." Samantha shook her head. "Yes, Walt made the right decision. I'm not even sure that I'm going to survive this."

"All right, we can handle it." Jo put her hands on her hips as she surveyed the space. "We'll just spend as much time as possible outside the cabin. All we need to do in here is sleep, right?" She tipped her head towards the built-in bunk beds. "I'll take the top one."

"Great." Samantha set her bag down on the bottom bunk. "I don't even want to imagine trying to climb up there in the middle of the night."

"Don't imagine it, let's go eat. They are supposed to be having brunch now." Jo smiled as she patted her stomach. "I was too nervous to eat anything this morning."

"You get nervous?" Samantha raised an eyebrow as she followed Jo out of the tiny cabin.

"Yes. Walt's not the only one that had some hesitation about being on this ship. I usually like to have an exit plan, wherever I am." Jo looked over the railing at the vast ocean water. "Doesn't seem like I do right now."

"Well, there are lifeboats." Samantha pointed to the boats that hung along the side of the ship.

"Good point." Jo took a deep breath. "That does make me feel a little better."

As they neared the restaurant serving brunch, Samantha laughed.

"It looks like Eddy's belly brought him to the same place." She pointed to Eddy as he approached the entrance of the restaurant.

"The food smells great." Eddy groaned as he led them inside. "I can't resist."

They settled at an empty table and ordered their food.

"I'm looking forward to some of the excursions." Samantha rubbed her hands together as she waited for the food to be served. "Tropical paradise, here I come!"

"They will be a lot of fun. Especially scuba diving." Jo smiled. "It's like getting a window into an entirely different world."

"Count me out on that one." Eddy shook his head. "I'm not planning on getting my feet wet on this trip. Just food, and relaxation, that's all I need."

"Here is a start." Their waitress smiled as she placed their plates on the table. "Enjoy!"

"Thank you." Samantha smiled at her as she hurried off. "The staff here are all so nice."

"Case in point." Jo tipped her head towards a young man she recognized as the same man that had taken her suitcase from Walt. He welcomed Carson and Annabella, the couple she had observed at the hotel bar the night before, with a friendly smile.

"Nick, it's good to see you again." Carson leaned on his cane. "I hope the food is as good as your service."

"You won't be disappointed, sir, I promise." Nick flashed a smile at him.

"It feels a little strange without Walt here." Samantha frowned as she pushed the food across her plate.

"Trust me, he is far happier at the hotel than he would be here." Jo looked up from her plate of food. "I'm sure he'd be horrified at the state of the kitchen."

"That's a good point." Eddy sat forward in his chair. "Although I can't complain about these eggs. They are delicious."

Eddy glanced up as Nick led Carson and Annabella to the table next to theirs.

"Are you sure there isn't somewhere less crowded we can eat?" Carson frowned as he glanced around at the bustling restaurant.

Eddy doubted that anyone on the cruise would turn down a free brunch, luckily there were several other restaurants on the ship that were offering the meal as well.

"Don't worry, sir, this is our best table." Nick pulled out a chair for Carson as he approached the table. "I will make sure that you get your food quickly, and that you're not disturbed."

"Wow, he really is working overtime for those tips." Samantha watched as the young man took Carson's cane and set it carefully to the side.

"Maybe the cruise line offers a little extra help to those that need it." Eddy glanced over as Annabella joined Carson at the table. "Although I haven't seen Annabella leave his side, yet."

"I guess she doesn't want to risk someone else getting their arms around Mr. Carson Moneybags." Jo laughed and picked up her piece of toast.

"Listen to us, we're worse than the gossipers at the diner back home." Eddy clucked his tongue. "It's not our place to judge, is it?"

"You're right it's not." Samantha sighed and blushed. "I just need more coffee."

"It's easy to say we shouldn't judge, but I've seen this so many times." Jo shook her head as she watched the pair. "I can't tell you how many circles I would run in where the trophy wives were young enough to be daughters to the men they called husbands."

"Were these the same circles that you conned and stole from?" Eddy leaned forward across the table and met Jo's eyes. "Wait, were you ever one of these women? A trophy wife, or girlfriend?"

"Eddy!" Samantha swatted at his arm. "Of course not."

"Not a chance." Jo pursed her lips. "Don't get me wrong, I know how hard these women work. It's no easy task. It really does come down to being a business arrangement in some cases, but the women have no legal avenue to pursue if the man changes his mind. Often, they become caregivers too, as the men become ill with age. They have the money to hire nurses, but much of the burden falls on these young women." She shrugged. "To each their own, I say, but I guess I'm a little more traditional when it comes to relationships. I think it's important to have a real emotional connection."

"I didn't know you were such a romantic, Jo." Eddy smiled as he ate the last bite of his eggs.

"Not a romantic exactly, I just believe that if you're going to spend the rest of your life with someone, it should be someone that you truly care about." Jo set down her fork which made a light clang against her plate. "Someone that you wouldn't want to be without."

"It's pretty easy to think you have found that."

Samantha frowned. "It doesn't always turn out that way, though."

"What are we doing talking about romance? We're here to have fun." Eddy grinned. "And romance isn't on my list of fun things."

"That I can believe." Samantha laughed as she met his eyes. "I don't think you have a romantic bone in your body."

"Ouch." Eddy winced, then smiled. "Sam, you have such a poor view of me."

"Not at all." Samantha winked at him. "I like you for exactly who you are."

"I can be romantic." Eddy narrowed his eyes as he studied her. "Do you really think I'm not capable?"

"I think, some things just aren't in your wheelhouse." Samantha shrugged.

"What does that even mean?" Eddy gazed at her.

"What are you doing on this ship, Carson?" A voice boomed from the middle of the restaurant. "You and I need to talk."

A man with silver hair and thick, broad shoulders stalked towards Carson's table.

CHAPTER 3

Eddy narrowed his eyes as he sensed the tension in the voice of the man who approached Carson. His instincts and experience warned him that things could easily get out of hand.

"Who is that?" Carson looked up, then squinted at the man who paused beside his table. "Bobby? Bobby McPherson? What are you doing here?"

"What am I doing here? What are you doing on my ship?" Bobby snarled each word. "You shouldn't be here!"

"This isn't your ship." Carson chuckled. "Just because you helped design it, doesn't mean that you own it. I bought a ticket, just like everyone else."

"You did it just to spite me." Bobby's hands balled into fists at his sides.

Eddy shifted in his chair.

"Easy." Samantha placed her hand on his forearm. "Give them a second to work it out."

"Excuse us, but we're enjoying our meal." Annabella glared at Bobby.

"I bet. Enjoy it while it lasts, Carson, because one of these days everyone is going to figure out that you're nothing more than a con artist." Bobby spun on his heel and walked away from the table. He continued right out of the restaurant.

"Sorry folks." Carson pulled off his bright red hat and set it on the table beside him.

"See?" Samantha shrugged as she looked back at her food. "Nothing to be concerned about."

"I wouldn't say that was nothing." Jo shook her head as she watched the couple at the next table. "Those two men obviously have some drama between them, and they are stuck on a ship together, that could certainly get messy."

"Yes, it could." Eddy narrowed his eyes.

"It's such a bright hat." Samantha eyed the hat on the table. "He has a unique fashion sense. I admire that in a man."

"He doesn't seem too disturbed." Jo shrugged, then she glanced at her watch. "Oops, I have to go. I promised Walt I would video chat with him after brunch."

"I thought we were exploring?" Eddy took the last swallow of his drink.

"I'll catch up with you." Jo waved to them, then headed out of the restaurant.

"I guess it's just you and me." Eddy looked across the table at Samantha. "I'm sorry if I don't meet your desire for a fashionable date."

"Oh stop." Samantha laughed as she stood up from the table. "Let's go see what interesting things we can find." She wrapped her arm around his and he led the way out of the restaurant.

Samantha glanced back over her shoulder at Annabella and Carson just as Annabella's gaze settled on a couple at another table. Samantha watched as Annabella continued to stare, then glanced swiftly away.

"Right this way, Sam. We have a lot of ship to cover." Eddy steered her around a crowd of people.

"Eddy, we really should go say hello to Walt first and make sure he's all right. Then we can check out the ship." Samantha tugged him back towards the cabin. "At least for a few minutes."

"We weren't invited." Eddy quirked an eyebrow.

"It's Walt and Jo, I think the invitation is always open." Samantha frowned as she met Eddy's eyes. "Is there some reason you don't want to talk to him?"

"It's not that I don't want to talk to him. I just feel bad, we're here, he's there, it feels a bit like we're rubbing it in." Eddy took a short breath. "But you're right, we should talk to him. It's too crowded out here to explore right now, anyway."

When they reached the cabin, Samantha gave a light knock on the door, then pushed it open.

"Look Walt, Eddy and Samantha are here." Jo grinned as she lifted her phone into the air.

"How are things going there, Walt?" Eddy squeezed his way into the small space.

"I have already begun to enjoy myself." Walt smiled into the camera. "I have plans to go for a walk soon. The weather is sunny, so I think that will be quite pleasant."

"It sounds like it will be." Samantha peered into the camera. "Just enjoy that spacious room. Did Jo show you how tiny our cabin is?"

"She did." Walt laughed. "I don't know how you can breathe in there. I know I wouldn't be able to."

"Please Walt, please for the sake of our friendship and my sanity do not tell me about mutated germs, or deadly diseases contracted due to living in a confined space." Samantha groaned.

"Ah Samantha, you know me far too well." Walt chuckled. "Perhaps I should just email over some helpful sites I've found?"

"Don't you do it, Walt." Samantha glowered into the camera.

"Well, I don't want to hold you three up, you should be out enjoying yourselves not holed up in that tiny little cabin. I'll check in with you tomorrow." Walt waved to them. "Have fun! Don't fall off the ship!"

"I'm more worried about these two throwing me off." Eddy grinned as he glanced at Jo and Samantha.

"Now, there's an idea." Samantha winked at him.

"Bye Walt." Jo waved to him, then hung up the phone. "I feel a little better now that I've talked to him."

"Good. Me too." Samantha eyed the cabin. "But honestly, if I don't get out of here soon, I think I'm going to break out in hives."

After several hours of exploring and trying out two different restaurants, Samantha was exhausted. The cruise was a great idea, but she didn't realize just how worn out she would be.

"I can't wait to crawl into bed." She yawned as she stepped into their cabin.

"Crawling might be what you have to do." Jo raised an eyebrow as she noted how low the bottom bunk was. "But let me climb up first." She pulled herself up onto the top bunk.

"I don't even care how small it is anymore, just that I have a soft place to put my head." Samantha stretched out in the bed and closed her eyes. A few hours later, her eyes snapped open. Her heart pounded against her chest, though she had no idea why. She was about to climb out of her bed, when Jo dropped down to the floor before she could.

"What is that?" Jo headed straight for the door of the cabin as a siren continued to blare.

"That's what woke me up." Samantha wiped her eyes. "Is it some kind of drill, or evacuation?" She followed Jo through the door.

"I'm not sure." Jo frowned as she led Samantha down the corridor. "But it's so loud, it must be some kind of emergency signal."

"Jo, Samantha!" Eddy stepped out of his cabin and rushed down the corridor towards them. "Who is it? Do we know?"

"Who is what?" Samantha looked over at him as she reached the steps that led up to the deck.

"That alarm is a signal that someone has fallen overboard." Eddy brushed past them and up the stairs.

As Samantha reached the top of the stairs the ship shuddered.

"That's it, they're slowing the ship down, and they'll be turning it back soon." Eddy walked towards the railing and peered over the edge. "It's so dark. They're going to have a hard time finding anyone."

"They have spotlights." Jo frowned as she looked out over the water. "That should help, shouldn't it?"

"I don't understand how anyone could fall off here." Samantha pursed her lips as she surveyed the railing. "Are you sure that's what the signal means?"

"I'm sure." Eddy nodded. "Even if they only suspect that someone went over, they will sound it. It's serious business. Either someone is in the water, or someone is missing, either way, someone is in trouble."

The PA system throughout the ship came alive with a stern voice.

"There is a report of a man overboard. Please remain in your cabins. Security will be conducting cabin-to-cabin and deck-to-deck searches for the next few hours, while we also conduct a search in the water. Please remain in your cabins so that the security team can conduct their search as quickly as possible. Thank you for your cooperation."

The voice cut off.

Jo looked over at Samantha. "Walt warned me about this." She shuddered. "I didn't really think it was possible."

"It is. It does happen." Eddy crossed his arms. "I certainly wasn't expecting it to happen on this trip, however. I guess with all the drinks that were flowing, someone must have gotten a little too drunk. And there is always the possibility that someone didn't fall but jumped." He cringed at the thought.

"But look at those railings." Jo patted the top of a railing that almost reached her chest. "They don't look that easy to climb."

"When someone is determined, they can do just about anything." Samantha watched as a group of security guards walked towards them. "We'd better get back to our cabins, so that they can conduct their search."

"You two go ahead." Eddy nodded. "I want to speak with the security guards and see if I can be of any help."

"Remember, you're retired, Eddy." Samantha gave his shoulder a light nudge.

"I remember, I'm just going to offer, I swear." Eddy walked towards the guards.

"Sir, we need you to return to your cabin." The guard that looked in charge paused in front of him. "It'll really help us with the search if the decks are clear."

"I understand, and I will go back to my cabin, but if you could use an extra pair of hands or eyes, I do have some experience with search and rescue. I'm a retired police officer. A detective." He offered his hand. "Eddy."

"Eddy, I'm Blake. I'm the head of the security guards. Thanks for the offer, but we've got it covered. Now, please return to your cabin."

"Sure, I'm on my way. If you need any assistance at all, please feel free to let me know. I'm in cabin three twenty-two."

"I'll keep that in mind." Blake pointed towards the corridor. "Quickly please."

"On my way." Eddy walked back towards his cabin. He shot a brief look over his shoulder at the young man. Was he even thirty? He doubted it. Somewhere around twenty-five he guessed. And he was in charge of the security guards? Eddy frowned as he knocked on the door to Samantha and Jo's cabin. "It's me Eddy."

"Eddy?" Jo pulled open the door. "How did the talk with the guards go?"

"They weren't interested in my help. But I can't shake the feeling that they might need it." Eddy shook his head. "I don't think I can wait it out here. There's just not enough room. I'll check in with you later. I'll go back to my cabin until I hear something." He started to walk down the passageway.

"It's probably for the best." Samantha started to close the door, when an ear-splitting shriek echoed down the corridor. She yanked the door back open and stepped out into the corridor with Jo right behind her. "Who was that?"

"It's Annabella." Eddy gazed down the corridor at Blake and Annabella who stood close together. Blake wrapped his arms around her to steady her.

"Do you think it's Carson that's missing?" Samantha gasped. Her heart began to race. Moments ago the missing person was a nameless, faceless passenger that she would likely never encounter. Now, she felt the urgency in the search. "He wouldn't be able to survive in that water long."

"It may be that he hasn't." Eddy tipped his head

towards the pair. "That seems like bad news."

The three watched as Blake walked away, and Annabella sank down on a bench.

"I'm going to see if she's all right." Samantha walked away before either of her friends could protest. She knew that she was supposed to stay in her cabin, and that inserting herself in the crisis had the potential to make things worse, but she couldn't stand the sight of the woman sitting all alone as her shoulders trembled with grief.

"Annabella, right?" Samantha sat down on the bench beside her. She offered a sympathetic frown.

"Do I know you?" Annabella blinked as she looked at Samantha.

"No, I don't think so. We were at the restaurant last night. I noticed you and Carson." Samantha put her hand on top of Annabella's. "I'm sorry, I know that this must be very difficult for you."

"I left him on the deck. When he wasn't in the cabin when I woke up, I just assumed he had fallen asleep on the deck. He was tired and had quite a bit to drink." Annabella wiped at her eyes. "But Blake just told me that they haven't been able to locate him on the ship. He's pretty convinced that he's in the water, but that's impossible."

"They are still searching on the ship. I'm sure he

just wanted to prepare you for the possibility." Samantha draped her arm around Annabella's shoulders. "Just take it one step at a time. I'm sure they'll find him tucked away in some corner of the ship somewhere."

"I'm sure he's fine." Annabella shivered as she took a deep breath. "He has to be fine. He must have just gotten himself stuck somewhere on the ship. Maybe locked in a storage room or something. Who knows! I told the security guard not to give the man overboard signal, that Carson would never be alone close to the railing, but he insisted. He said it is just in case, as the farther we get from where someone might have fallen, the less likely it is that they will find him. Oh!" She cupped her mouth as she gasped.

"It's okay to be scared." Samantha squeezed her hand and stroked the woman's back. "Just try to take a few breaths, Annabella. I'm sure that you're right. He'll be found very soon. Is he your husband, or your boyfriend?" She noticed that Annabella didn't have a ring on her finger.

"No, nothing like that." Annabella gulped and straightened up on the bench. "I'm just his assistant. I take care of whatever he might need and arrange his medications. I never should have left him alone on the deck! I should have stayed with him." She squeezed her eyes shut tight.

"It's not your fault, Annabella." Samantha stroked her back some more. Then she lowered her voice. "Annabella, I saw you two at the hotel bar last night. I saw you kiss. It's okay, you can tell me the truth."

"You did?" Annabella blushed and pulled her hand free of Samantha's. "Sometimes when Carson drinks, he gets a little confused. He doesn't like people to think that he needs someone to take care of him. So, he treats me like a girlfriend at times. But of course, we're not actually together." She wiped at her cheek as a tear slid down it. "Oh, he's gotten us into quite a mess this time."

"Do you think he overdid it tonight?" Samantha glanced down the corridor at Jo and Eddy who remained huddled close together.

"He wanted to celebrate. He was drinking more than usual. Now and then he'll drink until he passes out, but it's usually when we're at home." Annabella shook her head and held back a sob. "This is crazy. He's fine, I'm sure he's fine. He has to be fine!"

The siren wailed above them. Annabella turned into Samantha's arms and wept against her shoulder.

CHAPTER 4

"Enough of this." Eddy frowned as he watched Samantha embrace Annabella. "There's no reason for me to be stuck in my cabin when all eyes need to be involved in this search."

"Eddy, you could get us kicked off the ship." Jo frowned as she crossed her arms. "We were told to stay in our cabins."

"Do you care about that when someone is missing. Carson could be hurt." Eddy locked his eyes to hers. "I know you're no stickler for the rules."

"Fine, but if you're going to look, I'm going with you. I know you're no good at taking orders from anyone." Jo held his gaze.

"Fine, but let's be quiet about it." Eddy tipped

his head and raised his eyebrows towards Samantha to let her know his intentions. Then he started up the stairs to the main deck. He heard Jo's soft footsteps behind him. He knew she could be even quieter if she wanted to be. Her skills could come in handy if they had to avoid the security team. He walked over to the railing and looked over the side of the ship. "It's so far down." He gave a low whistle, then glanced at Jo.

"Too far." Jo pursed her lips. "He would have had plenty of time to scream. Someone would have heard him."

"Even if they were all in their cabins?" Eddy tipped his head back and forth.

"We heard Annabella scream. I'm sure that there were other people still on the deck. No one wants to go to bed early on a cruise." Jo glanced back towards the steps. "Especially in cabins that small."

"You're probably right about that." Eddy squinted as he looked out over the water. "But that doesn't mean that anyone will come forward about hearing him scream."

"Why wouldn't they?" Jo asked. "Someone's life is in danger, why wouldn't they say anything?"

"Jo, look." Eddy pointed towards one of the

lifeboats on the side of the ship. "Something looks off about that one, doesn't it?"

"One side is slightly lower than the other." Jo nodded. "Do you think he might have hit it on the way down?"

"It could be a clue." Eddy looked up at the sound of footsteps headed in their direction. "I'll let Blake know. They might need to concentrate their search in this area."

"Eddy." Jo's voice was sharp despite how softly she spoke.

"Jo?" Eddy looked over at her, his heart in his throat. He sensed from her demeanor that something was very wrong.

"Eddy. Is that a foot?" Jo pointed to the lifeboat and what looked like toes poking out from beneath the orange tarp that covered part of the open section on the top of it.

"No, it can't be." Eddy's voice shuddered as he stared. He wanted it to be something else, anything else, but the more he looked at it, the more he believed Jo was right. "Blake!" He waved his arms at the security guard. "Blake, over here!"

"I thought I told you to stay in your cabin?" Blake frowned as he jogged the remaining distance between them.

"Listen, son." Eddy's gaze riveted to Blake's. "You're about to have a lot more on your plate to worry about than a couple of people not following orders. Take a look at what is in that lifeboat down there." He jabbed his finger over the railing in the direction of the lifeboat.

"What?" Blake peered over the railing. "I don't see anything."

"And that's exactly why you need my help." Eddy rolled his eyes. He gestured to the flashlight on Blake's belt. "Why don't you use that and have another look?"

"I really don't have time for these games." Blake frowned, but pulled his flashlight from his hip. He shined it down towards the lifeboat. A second later his flashlight splashed into the water. "Oh no." He stumbled back from the railing. "That's what I think it is, isn't it?" He looked at Eddy with wide eyes.

"I believe so, yes. But you won't know for sure until someone gets down there, or you pull the boat up." Eddy regarded him with some frustration. "Blake, are you with me here?"

"I'm sorry." Blake cleared his throat. "I've never had anything like this happen before. The chief and deputy security officers for the ship are sick in their cabins. They have some sort of bug. I've never dealt

CRUISES CAN BE DEADLY

with anything like this before." He cringed as he peered over the side of the ship once more.

"You're going to need to get your men together and get that boat up here so that the body can be examined, and we can confirm the identity of the victim." Eddy eyed the boat again. "Then you're going to have to figure out how that victim ended up under a tarp. Son, you don't just have a body on your hands, you probably have a murder."

"Don't say that." Blake took a step back. "We don't know that yet. He could still be alive. It could still be an accident." He pulled out his radio and barked into it, summoning the other guards.

Eddy stepped off to the side. Jo followed after.

"Does he really believe that it could be an accident?" Jo rolled her eyes, then watched as the other men gathered around him. "What are they discussing? They need to get the boat up here."

"Take a breath, Jo. There really isn't any need to rush. It's not as if he's taking a nap in there." Eddy frowned. "There's no way that he could have climbed down the side of the ship and crawled into the boat himself. I think there must be foul play involved. I think he was most likely murdered."

"That means that if he was killed, someone else would have had to get him down there."

"Or get the boat up here and him inside."

"Eddy." Jo gripped the railing and took a slow breath. "That means that we're on this ship with a murderer."

"That's possible." Eddy nodded and glanced over at her. "It's also possible that whoever did this might have already jumped ship. But it would probably be simpler for whoever did this to blend in with the crowd."

"It's like a small city on this ship. There are hundreds of people on board. How are we ever going to narrow it down?" Jo skimmed her gaze over the length of the ship that she could see. She knew there was much more that she couldn't.

"If he was murdered, I doubt a perfect stranger would go to this much trouble." Eddy narrowed his eyes. "My hunch is that whoever did this to Carson, did it for a personal reason."

"Are we sure it's him?" Jo shifted her attention to Blake who spoke to the other guards.

Eddy and Jo watched the men but couldn't hear what they were saying. The security guards began to draw the lifeboat up to the level of the deck.

Jo trained her attention on the security guards as they began to examine the lifeboat. Her heart skipped a beat as for just a second, she hoped it all might be a mistake. Maybe it was some kind of dummy? Or maybe Carson really had managed to get into the boat to take a nap.

Blake looked up from the boat, and over to Eddy, his skin pale and his eyes wide. His lips tightened into a grimace as he looked back at the boat.

"I'm pretty sure it's him." Eddy crossed his arms as he watched the four men carefully remove the tarp. "I also think they are in far over their heads."

"What is the procedure when something like this happens?" Jo watched as staff from the ship's medical center walked towards the boat. Walked. There was no urgency in their pace.

"I'm not sure exactly, but I would assume that a team will be sent out to the ship to investigate. We're a day away from any land, so it may take some time." Eddy glanced at his watch. "I think we're in for a long night."

Jo heaved a heavy sigh as the weight of the night's revelation washed over her. They were no longer on a vacation. She sensed it in the way Eddy's eyes tightened, in the way Samantha's arm had been curved around Annabella's shoulders, and in the pounding of her own heart. None of them would be able to let this go, until they found out what happened to Carson.

"How do you think Annabella's going to take it?" Eddy frowned.

"I'm sure it won't be easy news for her to receive."

"Unless it's news she's expecting." Eddy quirked an eyebrow as he looked at Jo.

"You think she might have had something to do with this?" Jo met his eyes.

"As of now, everyone on this ship is a suspect." Eddy pulled his phone from his pocket and sent a text to Samantha to confirm what they had found. "I'm going to get an update from Blake. Maybe you should join Sam. See if you can get a clear read on Annabella's reaction when she hears the news."

"I'll do that." Jo nodded and started to walk away, then paused and looked back at Eddy. "Be careful, Eddy, don't push too hard, or you might end up tossed off the ship."

"I'll be fine." Eddy turned and walked towards the security guards. As he did, Blake began to walk towards him.

"Eddy, you were right." Blake paused in front of Eddy. "It's the missing passenger."

"Carson?" Eddy frowned as he looked past

Blake, towards the lifeboat. "How was he killed?"

"He was strangled, it looks like, but I can't be sure. He is dressed, but some of his clothes, like his shoes, are missing." Blake shook his head. "I've never dealt with anything like this."

"Just take it one step at a time, Blake."

"The captain has instructed me to secure the boat and the body."

"That sounds right, you don't want anyone to be able to interfere with the evidence that you do have."

"The captain will inform the authorities. And the ship's doctor will inform Annabella." Blake swallowed hard.

"That's good, at least you don't have to deal with that." Eddy tipped his head towards the other security guards. "Make sure that the security guards understand it's important to keep the details of the crime scene to themselves. Those tiny details could be the factor that proves a suspect is a killer, instead of just a suspect."

"Suspect." Blake took a deep breath and blew it out into the air between them. "I can't even begin to think about that."

"You're going to have to." Eddy put his hand on Blake's shoulder and met his eyes. "But I can help you. If you want me to, until the proper authorities get here."

"They're not coming." Blake cleared his throat. "The captain already contacted them when Carson went missing. There's a bad storm due to strike us. They can't risk sending someone out here now. We were supposed to be ahead of it, but since we stopped the ship to look for Carson, it's closer, and the latest weather reports say that it's sped up." He ran his hand along the back of his neck. "We are trying to avoid it, but unless something changes, it's just going to be us, until we're able to dock at the next port. I can't believe the security officers aren't well enough to deal with this. Eddy, I have no idea what I'm doing here. I am only new to the job. A man overboard, I know the procedure for. A storm hitting the ship, I know what to do in that situation, too. But a murder on board?" He shook his head slowly. "I know the steps to take, but I've never had to execute them."

"Lucky for you, you have an experienced detective on your ship." Eddy managed a small smile. "I'll do my best to help you."

"I am not looking forward to Annabella being informed that Carson is deceased." Blake wrung his hands. "At least the doctor will inform her. I'm afraid I'll say something wrong and make things worse for her. She told me how close they were, and when I said that I couldn't find him on the ship, she screamed like you would not believe."

"I heard it." Eddy nodded slowly. "Tell the other guards to secure the boat and the body."

"Okay." Blake wrung his hands as he hesitated.

Eddy watched as Blake hurried back over to the other guards. He did his best to be patient. Blake was young, he'd likely taken the job as a way to travel and make some good money, without having to deal with much more than drunken passengers and the occasional nasty weather. Instead he was faced with a rather unique homicide.

Eddy did his best not to roll his eyes. He didn't expect a lot from Blake, but his nervousness left him unsettled. What if there had been a crisis that impacted the entire ship? Would he have been able to handle that?

When Blake returned to Eddy's side, he appeared a little more determined. The doctor walked along the deck towards Blake.

"Let's go talk to Annabella."

"All right, I'm ready." Blake nodded. Eddy followed after them at a distance. He wanted to see Annabella's reaction.

Blake slowed and walked with Eddy as the doctor took the lead.

"Just remember, grief can make people react in very strange ways. Make sure you're ready for anything." Eddy told Blake as they walked towards Annabella.

"I will be." Blake put his hand on the bottle of pepper spray in his belt.

"No, not that, Blake. You're not going to pepper spray a grieving woman, got it?" Eddy glared at him.

"Well, I just thought, you know if she—"

"Just be ready to grab her, hug her, keep her from doing something crazy. Not hurt her." Eddy frowned, shook his head, then walked towards Annabella, stopping a few feet away. He stood to the side as the doctor walked up to Annabella.

Jo and Samantha looked up at him as he walked over. Annabella's gaze flitted between the doctor, and Blake and Eddy who stood behind him, her expression a mixture of hope and fear.

Eddy wished the doctor didn't have to deliver the news, but he knew the longer he waited the more painful it would be.

"Annabella." The doctor stood in front of her.

"Carson, where is he? Did you find him?"

Annabella looked from the doctor, to Blake, to Eddy then back to the doctor again.

"Yes, we found him. Unfortunately, Carson has passed away." The doctor reached out to take her hand, but she jerked it away before he could. "I'm very sorry for your loss, Annabella."

"I'm so sorry." Samantha tightened her grasp on Annabella's shoulder.

"No!" Annabella shot up off the bench. "No, you're wrong! He can't be dead! I want to see him!"

"Ma'am, you can't do that just yet." Blake stepped in front of her.

"Of course, I can! I demand to see him!" Annabella started to push past Blake.

"Annabella." Jo caught her by the arm and pulled her back. "Just take a deep breath."

"Who are you people to tell me to do anything?" Annabella shook her arm free of Jo's grasp.

"It's important that the security staff be able to conduct their investigation, Annabella." Blake took a step closer to her. "Don't you want to know what happened to Carson?"

"What do you mean, what happened to him?" Annabella took a sharp breath. "Didn't he fall overboard?"

CHAPTER 5

Samantha stood beside Annabella, ready to catch the woman if she collapsed. She knew from experience that adrenaline could run out in a second and turn into exhaustion. When she'd investigated tragic stories in the past, she'd seen grief take on many forms, and Annabella was certainly caught up in a tragedy. The text from Eddy that revealed that Carson was dead, and had likely been killed, jolted her out of her dazed state and made her realize that even though Annabella barely knew her, she was going to need Samantha to be a friend.

"No, he didn't fall overboard." Blake spoke up and took a step closer to her. "We are investigating right now. We will find out exactly what happened."

"I don't understand." Annabella frowned. "Why aren't you being clear with me? What happened to him? Was it some kind of accident?"

"At this time, we can't be sure." The doctor looked into her eyes. "The best thing you can do is get some rest and let the security team investigate."

"This is insane." Annabella shook her head and turned away from them. "There's no way this could be true. I must be dreaming. This is just a dream." She ran her hands across her face.

"I'm sorry, it isn't. I'll leave you in the capable hands of Blake so I can see to matters of urgency." The doctor spoke gently to Annabella. "Please let the crew know if you need anything." He turned and walked towards the stairs.

"Annabella, I'm Eddy. I am very sorry for your loss." Eddy stepped around her so that he could watch her expression as she replied. "Annabella, what was Carson doing the last time you saw him?"

"He was on the deck, on one of the loungers. I told him I wanted to go to the bar, have a drink. But he was comfortable, he didn't want to move. He told me to go ahead, and that he'd meet me back at the cabin. So, I went to the bar, and when I came back to the cabin, he wasn't there. I figured he wanted a little more time on the deck, so I got into bed. I didn't mean to doze off. I was going to go check on him if he wasn't back soon. But when I woke up a few hours later, he was still not in the cabin. That's when I panicked. I went out to the lounger, and he wasn't there. That's when I alerted security." She sank back down onto the bench. "Oh, I never should have left him alone! Why did I do that? Why did I leave him alone?" Her voice grew louder as tears spilled down her cheeks. "Why didn't I just stay with him?"

"It's not your fault, Annabella." Samantha sat back down beside her and took her hand. "You couldn't have known."

"She's right." Jo sat down on the other side of her. "There's no reason to blame yourself. But anything you can tell us about Carson could help us to figure out what happened here."

"I can't." Annabella shuddered as she began to rock back and forth on the bench. "Oh, what am I going to tell his family? Oh no, this can't be true." She gasped as she closed her eyes.

"I can help you contact them if you'd like." Samantha pulled her phone out of her pocket. "Why don't we go back to your cabin? Or if you'd prefer, we could go to my cabin?"

"No, I'm not going anywhere until I find out

what happened to Carson." Annabella stood up again, and this time marched straight towards Blake. "You have no right to withhold that information from me. Either you tell me now or I will make sure that you are fired, do you understand me?" She pointed her finger directly at his face as she continued. "I will make sure that you never work in this position again. I am not kidding. I do not play games!"

"All right, all right!" Blake held his hands up in the air. "He was strangled, okay?"

"Blake!" Eddy growled and stepped between Blake and Annabella. "We don't know that yet, Annabella, not for sure."

"Strangled." Annabella wobbled where she stood. "You mean that he was killed?" Her voice grew high and trembled. "Someone killed him?"

"Easy." Samantha caught her by the elbow while Jo stood behind her, prepared to steady her if needed.

"Murdered?" Annabella blinked as fresh tears slid down her cheeks. "How could that happen? Who would do this?"

"That's what we're going to find out." Eddy assured her, then shot a sharp look in Blake's direction. "Blake, why don't you come with me?"

"Right, sure." He nodded, then followed after Eddy.

"Annabella, are you okay?" Samantha gently steered her back down onto the bench. She noticed the woman's stricken expression and the way her mouth remained partly open, though she didn't speak. It seemed like genuine shock to her.

"Maybe we should get the nurse." Jo stood up from the bench.

"No, it's all right." Annabella's shoulders slumped. "It's all right. I don't need the nurse." She shivered. "I think I just need to lay down for a little while. I'll call Carson's family in the morning. It won't make a difference will it? It's the middle of the night." She glanced up at the sky. "Or almost morning I guess, isn't it?"

"It's nearly three." Jo frowned as she helped Annabella to her feet. "It's probably a good idea to get some rest."

"I'll get her settled." Samantha tipped her head towards Eddy and Blake. "You should probably keep an eye on that situation."

"Yes, you're right." Jo winced as she watched Eddy jab his finger into his palm again and again while speaking to Blake. "It looks like he might need a little help."

Samantha led Annabella back to her cabin. As she eased open the door, she was stunned by what she saw inside. It was easily three times the size of the cabin that she and Jo shared. Instead of bunk beds there was a double bed. A door on the side of the cabin indicated that there was a separate bathroom, which she guessed contained both a shower and a toilet instead of a combination of the two.

"This is my cabin." Annabella sighed. "Carson's is the adjoining cabin." She walked towards a door and opened it. Samantha looked inside and was shocked to find that this cabin was even bigger. It had what looked like a king-sized bed and a separate bathroom.

"Oh Carson!" Annabella gasped as she looked around the cabin. "How could this be true?"

Samantha noticed a suitcase open on the side of the bed. It contained men's dress shirts and trousers from what she could see. There was also a stack of books on the table beside the bed. Each one had to do with investment.

"I know it's overwhelming, Annabella. It's okay, whatever you need to say, whatever you need to do, I'm here to help you." Samantha guided her back towards her bed.

"You shouldn't stay." Annabella sank down on her bed. "Just go." She turned her head into her pillow.

"It's all right, Annabella, I don't mind staying." Samantha lingered beside the bed.

"No, please. I'd rather you didn't. I know you're trying to be kind, but I need some time alone." Annabella tried to hold back a sob.

"I understand." Samantha swept her gaze around the cabin one more time. She looked for anything that would indicate who might want to harm Carson. However, the evidence was sparse. He hadn't even unpacked, and she couldn't exactly dig through Carson's suitcase with Annabella there to see. "If you need anything at all, please let me know, Annabella." She jotted her phone number down on a pad of paper on the table beside Annabella's bed. "I'll be back to check on you later."

"Sure, thanks," Annabella muttered, then trembled as another sob traveled through her.

As Samantha stepped out of the cabin, she felt a need to protect her rush through her. Though she didn't know Annabella well, and though she didn't have children of her own, for some reason she felt a maternal drive to keep her safe and a fierce anger towards whoever had caused her so much pain. As she walked down the corridor, a little startled by her emotional reaction, she spotted Eddy and Jo near Eddy's cabin.

Eddy shifted from one foot to the other as he watched Samantha approach. His conversation with Blake had revealed more than he anticipated, and he looked forward to sharing the information with Jo and Samantha, but in particular Samantha. Whenever he faced a problem, he couldn't find a solution to, she managed to figure it out for him.

"Samantha, did you notice anything off in Annabella's cabin?" Jo asked.

"Nothing, other than the fact that her cabin was adjoining Carson's and they are both huge." Samantha shook her head. "If I ever decide to go on a cruise again, I'm going to make sure that I get a cabin like that."

"I managed to get some information from Blake." Eddy opened his cabin door and followed them inside, then pulled the door closed behind him. "I'm not sure that it will help us figure much out but it's a start."

"What do you have?" Samantha sat down on the edge of the bottom bunk bed.

"There's surveillance video of Carson going back

to his cabin." Eddy perched on the small chair in the room, while Jo sat down next to Samantha. "Blake let me take a look. It's him, with his purple scarf and his ivory cane, and that red hat. There's no mistaking him for someone else."

"What does this mean?" Jo frowned. "He wasn't on the deck?"

"Yes. At least, not when he was attacked. It means he went back to his cabin before he was killed." Eddy shook his head. "It explains why no one heard the attack. If he was in his cabin when he was killed, even if he fought back, it's possible no one would have heard him."

"But what about Annabella?" Samantha frowned. "She would have heard him."

"If she was there." Jo narrowed her eyes. "Maybe she wasn't. Or maybe she was." She looked up at Eddy. "Maybe she is the only one who knows what happened."

"You mean if she killed him?" Samantha sat forward on the bunk bed. "I don't think that's possible."

"Anything is possible. Right now, anyway. Now we know that someone didn't confront him on the deck. They took him from his cabin. And like Eddy said, they likely killed him there. But someone still carried him out to that lifeboat." Jo stood up from the bunk bed. "That would have taken a bit of strength, and certainly the person had to be smart enough to go undetected." She turned towards the cabin door. "Are there cameras in the corridors?"

"No, there are no cameras near the cabins for privacy reasons." Eddy raised his eyebrows. "Or so they can save money and avoid lawsuits. Either way, we don't know for sure that he went into his cabin and we don't have any proof that anyone took him back out."

"But we know he ended up in that lifeboat." Jo pursed her lips. "Under a tarp. Someone put his body there."

"Yes, that's true, but now we can't just narrow down the suspects to people that were on that deck at the time. It could have just as easily been any of the passengers that were on the cabin levels." Eddy pulled his hat off and frowned. "There are so many people on this ship, it might be impossible to narrow it down."

"But not all of those people would go to all of this trouble just to kill someone." Jo snapped her fingers. "We need Walt's help with this. He can at least find out a little bit more about Carson's financial history and whether there is anything there that might be able to steer us in a certain direction." She pulled out her phone. "I can set up a video chat with him right now."

"That sounds perfect." Eddy nodded.

"What about Carson himself?" Samantha met Eddy's eyes. "Did they find anything on his body or in the boat that might give us a clue?"

"The most unusual thing they found is what they didn't find." Eddy pulled a small notebook out of his pocket and began to look through it. "According to Blake, Carson was barefoot, he had pants, and his shirt, but his blazer was missing as was his hat, and his cane."

"Were those clothing items found in his cabin? What about his scarf?" Samantha touched her neck as she recalled the brightly colored accessory that Carson wore.

"There's nothing about the scarf, so I would assume that it wasn't there either, but Blake could have overlooked that." Eddy made a note on the notepad. "I'll ask him about it. I haven't gotten an account of what was or wasn't in the cabin. I think that will take some time."

"Walt is looking Carson up right now." Jo set

her phone down on the small table beside Eddy's chair so that they could all see it.

"Hi Walt." Eddy waved to him.

"Not now, working." Walt's voice was almost drowned out by the tapping of keys.

"It wouldn't be surprising for him to have taken all of those things off when he was in his cabin." Samantha tipped her head from side to side. "So, that leans more towards him being back in his cabin, and relaxing, when someone attacked him. Which also makes me think that he likely let the person into the cabin, and if he did that, then he probably knew the person."

"Who would he let into his cabin?" Jo settled back on the bunk bed beside Samantha.

"Certainly Annabella." Eddy made a note on the paper again. "He wouldn't suspect her presence at all. They have adjoining cabins."

"True, but who else?" Samantha narrowed her eyes. "Maybe that guy, Nick, the one with the braces?" Samantha raised an eyebrow. "He was helping out Carson left and right, Carson wouldn't have hesitated to let him in."

"That's a good point." Eddy nodded and made another note on the paper. "There's always Bobby, too, we can't rule him out."

"But would Carson have let him into his cabin? It didn't seem as if they were too friendly with each other." Jo crossed her arms.

"Maybe Bobby offered to reconcile?" Samantha looked over the notes on her phone. "Maybe he claimed to want to bury the hatchet and instead decided to end Carson's life?"

"It's definitely possible. But I'd be more inclined to believe that Bobby would just try to throw Carson off the side of the ship." Jo smiled.

"Maybe Bobby forced his way in." Eddy jotted down a few more things on his notepad. "At this point we can assume that we have three main suspects, but the truth is that it really could have been anyone on this ship. We don't know for sure that Carson knew the person that killed him."

"You're right, we don't." Samantha frowned. "In fact, the only thing that we do know for sure is that someone put him in that lifeboat, someone killed him."

"We also know something else." Walt's voice drifted from the phone on the table.

Samantha jumped, as she had forgotten for a moment that Walt was even on the video chat.

"What do you mean, Walt?" She peered at the phone. "Did you find something?"

"I think so." Walt looked into the camera and took a deep breath. "Carson was no ordinary man, that's for sure."

"Let's hear it." Eddy rested his elbows on his knees and leaned forward.

CHAPTER 6

Walt shifted in his chair until he felt content with the way his image looked in the camera.

"Can you all see me?"

"Yes," the others replied.

"Can you all hear me?"

"Walt?" Samantha laughed. "How could we have answered the first question if we couldn't hear you?"

"I'm just being thorough, Samantha." Walt frowned. "Now, pay close attention because our connection may not be stable."

"We're listening." Eddy nodded, his eyes locked to the screen. "Tell us what you found."

"To begin with, our victim Carson, he's not just a

wealthy guy with a penchant for fashion. He's a billionaire, who has had his hands in all kinds of businesses. From what I can tell he didn't actually work much in his life, instead he made his money off investing in, and buying up businesses, just to resell them for a profit. He's rarely owned any business longer than six months."

"It sounds like he's a bit of a genius." Jo pursed her lips. "You don't build up that kind of net worth without having a special talent for numbers and business."

"I can agree with that." Walt nodded, then cleared his throat. "But what makes Carson even more unique, is that he has no direct heirs. From what I've seen he hasn't ever been married, or shared assets with a woman or a man."

"Interesting." Jo glanced at the others. "I think that might have changed."

Walt looked into the camera and raised an eyebrow.

"That might explain Annabella's interest in Carson," Eddy agreed.

"I don't know." Samantha scrunched up her nose as she recalled the reaction that Annabella had when Carson's body was found. "I asked her about the kiss she and Carson shared. She claims that he does that when he's had a few drinks, or he wants people to believe that they are a couple, but they weren't actually together. I'm not sure that I believe her, though."

"Whether or not they were in a relationship it would be pretty easy for her to stay motivated as his companion if she stood to benefit from his wealth." Eddy rubbed his hand along his chin. "We may all think differently, but the truth is that she might have a strong motive to be behind this murder."

"But physically, do you think she could have pulled it off?" Jo shook her head. "I'm not so sure about that. She doesn't look that strong."

"Looks can be deceiving. I wouldn't look at you and automatically assume you could rappel down from a ceiling, but you can, can't you?" Eddy looked over at her.

"I suppose you're right, but I've never done it with the body of a grown man in tow." Jo stood up and began to pace back and forth in the tiny cabin. "What we need is a witness. Someone had to have seen something. It seems impossible to think that anyone could have pulled this off without being seen."

"Actually, that's a good point." Samantha stood up and began to pace with her. "It means that whoever did this likely did their research, or already had a pretty good working knowledge of the ship."

"Someone like Bobby?" Eddy looked up at both of them. "Didn't Carson say he designed this ship?"

"Bobby who?" Walt leaned closer to the camera. "Can you hear me? Are you still there?"

"Yes, we're still here." Samantha sat down on the bottom bunk. "Bobby McPherson. I think that's what Carson called him. He seemed to have a problem with Carson as well."

"I'll see what I can dig up on him." Walt sat back and began to type. "I'll have to get in touch with you later."

Before anyone could say goodbye, the video chat cut off.

"He's hard at work now." Jo sighed as she ran her hands back through her hair. "Hopefully, he can find something, but I'm not convinced that Bobby was involved. I mean, I still say there's a good chance that Annabella had something to do with it. Maybe she even hired someone else to commit the crime." Jo raised an eyebrow. "Someone stronger, someone who knows the ship fairly well. Maybe someone that works on it?"

"But why would she? As of now, she has a pretty good life taking care of Carson. She gets to go on luxury cruises and I'm guessing live in a mansion or at least a very nice house. Why would she want any of that to end?" Samantha stood up from the bunk bed and stretched out her arms.

"She did say he likes to pretend they are together, maybe it bothered her to the point that she wanted to get rid of him permanently. Maybe, he has insisted on taking things too far." Jo crossed her arms. "I don't know for sure of course. But in these cases, the person closest to the victim tends to be the one who committed the crime."

"That's true." Samantha sighed. "I guess it points us back in the same direction really, whether someone did it themselves, or someone hired someone to do it, the person who did it, probably had a good amount of knowledge about the ship. Maybe we should take a closer look at the crew."

"I think we should start with Bobby." Eddy glanced at his watch. "I think I'll have a run at him. Let me know if you hear from Walt, okay?"

"Will do." Samantha nodded as the three stepped out into the corridor.

Jo leaned close to Samantha as Eddy walked away.

"I hope you don't think I was picking on you about Annabella being a suspect."

"I don't think that at all. You have to trust your instincts, and I have to trust mine. I just hope one of us figures out what happened to Carson." Samantha gazed at the sky as they mounted the last of the steps to the deck. "Hopefully, before this storm washes away any possible evidence."

"Look at those clouds." Jo walked over to the railing. "I'd say we're really in for it."

"Do you think we'll be safe out here in the middle of the ocean?" Samantha's stomach churned at the thought of the ship capsizing.

"These ships are designed to weather a storm, I'm sure we'll be fine." Jo flashed a smile in her direction.

Samantha noticed that it didn't reach her friend's eyes. She might pretend to always be calm and in control, but she sensed that Jo was just as concerned about inclement weather and what it might do to the giant ship.

"I think I'll go have a conversation with Nick. I'm sure the staff has heard about what happened by now, and soon everyone on the ship will be aware of it as they wake up. Better to talk to him now before he has too much time to get his story straight."

"That's a good idea, Sam." Jo continued to gaze

out at the sky. "I'll let you do that. I'm going to see what I can find out as well."

"From who?" Samantha watched her calm expression.

"Good luck with Nick." Jo smiled at her, then turned and walked away.

Samantha was certain that Jo had heard her question, and yet she had chosen not to answer. She didn't have time to dwell on why. She needed to find Nick before he got swept up in the duties of his day.

Despite the cloudy sky, Eddy found Bobby right where he expected him to be. The tall man was stretched out in a lounger with his phone in one hand and a bottle of beer on the table beside him. Eddy guessed that the bars on the cruise ship didn't care what time it was when they started serving alcohol. He took the lounger next to Bobby's, despite the fact that there were many other empty chairs.

Bobby looked over at him, his eyes narrowed.

"Hi there." Eddy smiled at him. "It's nice to see another person who isn't scared off by a bit of rain."

"It's not raining, yet." Bobby spoke in a clipped

tone and shifted the phone in his hand. "I was just looking for a little peace and quiet."

Eddy grinned, as if he couldn't grasp the clear hint that Bobby gave to indicate that he didn't want to be bothered.

"I can understand that. You must be traveling with your wife, huh?" Eddy chuckled. "Those gals, they never leave you alone."

"My wife?" Bobby scoffed. "Hardly. I never travel with my wife. She has her own life, I have mine." He squinted at Eddy. "Did you have a few too many already this morning?"

"Not a drop, actually." Eddy pulled off his fedora and ran his hand back over his hair. "I guess honestly, I could use some coffee."

"Great, there's a café just down that corridor." Bobby pointed to the right.

"It can wait." Eddy shrugged. "I haven't had a decent conversation with anyone since I boarded this ship."

"I have a lot to do." Bobby shot a brief look of irritation in Eddy's direction, then turned his attention back to his phone.

"A lot to do when you are on a cruise?" Eddy shook his head and smiled. "Isn't this supposed to be a vacation? You've got to unwind sometime, pal."

"No, I don't actually. My work is always at my fingertips." Bobby sat up in his lounger and looked over at Eddy. "When you are in my line of work you always have a lot to do. Even on vacation. Don't you know what that's like?"

"Actually, I wouldn't know." Eddy shrugged as he stretched his legs out on the lounger. "I'm retired. It's all play and no work for me."

"Really?" Bobby turned some to get a better look at Eddy. "You don't look like the type to play. To me you look more like someone who never stops working. What did you retire from?"

"I was a detective." Eddy winked at him. "Badge and gun and all. It was great. But, when I was done, I was done."

"I find that hard to believe." Bobby cracked a smile for the first time. "I imagine you were actually quite reluctant to retire."

"Yes, you're right." Eddy chuckled. "It was the last thing I wanted. But it was time for me to hang it all up. I can see that now." He raised an eyebrow. "Could you imagine an old man like me trying to solve crimes?"

"Eh, I suppose not." Bobby leaned back against his lounger again. "In some cases, I do think that people should retire, however that shouldn't stop you from making money. Invest, invest, that's what I always say. Make your money work for you."

"Is that so?" Eddy glanced over at him. "I don't know too much about any of that."

"I could teach you a thing or two. But." Bobby tipped his head towards the phone in his hand. "I already have my hands full managing my own investments."

"Is that what you and Carson were involved in? Some kind of investment?" Eddy looked over at him, his eyes narrowed.

"Excuse me?" Bobby stood up from the lounger so suddenly that it scraped across the deck. "What are you bringing him up for?"

"I'm bringing him up because I noticed that argument you had with him in the restaurant. I don't think anyone there didn't notice it. It was a little bit dramatic, don't you think?" Eddy stood up as well.

"Is this some kind of game you're playing with me?" Bobby crossed his arms. "You acted like you had no idea who I was and now I find out that you were spying on me in the restaurant last night."

"I wasn't spying on you. You made your business very public." Eddy slid his hands into his pockets. "I was just there to observe it, like everyone else. I imagine though, that after what happened, you're feeling pretty guilty about the way you talked to him."

"After what happened?" Bobby took a step towards him. "What are you talking about?"

"Oh, you don't know? I thought you would have heard about it by now." Eddy rocked back on his heels. "They found old Carson in the middle of the night, dead as a doornail."

"Dead?" Bobby stumbled back, then caught his leg on his lounger. He fell down into a sitting position on it. "Are you sure?"

"I'm sure." Eddy studied the tension in his expression.

"What happened? A heart attack or something?" Bobby looked up at Eddy, his eyes wide.

"No, nothing like that." Eddy stepped closer until he stood right over him. "Carson was murdered."

Bobby took a sharp breath, then gripped the cushion on the lounger.

"Here, on the ship?"

"Where else?" Eddy quirked an eyebrow. "Are you all right there? You seem a little wobbly."

"How could this happen?" Bobby rested his head in his hands. "How could a murder happen on this ship? And it was Carson?" He snatched up his phone and began to type on it. "I've got to get ahead of this. As soon as word gets out, everything is going to be chaos."

"I guess saying I'm sorry for your loss wouldn't be appropriate?" Eddy gritted his teeth as he watched the man continue to type.

"Sure, Carson is dead, it's a great loss. He wasn't a terrible man, he wasn't a great man. But that doesn't mean that I don't need to get ahead of this before it turns into a disaster. Excuse me." Bobby stood up and walked back towards the steps that led to the cabins.

Eddy watched him go. He wasn't sure of the man's reaction. At first, he seemed shocked, and maybe even grief-stricken, but a second later he was lost in his phone, not to call friends or mutual acquaintances, but for personal reasons. To protect his reputation and himself from any potential financial loss. Would he really put on such a show if he had been the one to kill Carson?

The wind howled around the ship. Eddy looked up at the sky. It had grown quite a bit darker. He spotted Blake as he hurried past him.

"Blake! This storm is really picking up." Eddy

caught up with Blake as he reached the steps that led to the next level.

"It's going to get worse." Blake frowned as he looked down at Eddy. "It's going to be at least a day until the proper investigators can get here. I'm sorry, I have to go, Eddy, I have some more interviews to do."

Eddy nodded, then watched as Blake continued up the steps. Without reinforcements it was even less likely that the murder would be solved.

CHAPTER 7

Samantha didn't have to ask too many people before she found her way to Nick. He seemed to be a popular staff member.

"Oh Nick, he'll be down by the storage room. He usually handles inventory." A young woman directed her to the level and corridor that he would be in.

"Thanks so much." Samantha smiled at her, then followed the directions that she gave. As predicted, Nick stood right beside the door of a storage room. He rummaged in his pocket for something.

"Hi. Nick, right?" Samantha paused beside him.

"Yes, I'm Nick." He looked at her. "Did you need help with something?"

"Actually, I just need a few minutes of your time.

Would that be possible?" Samantha noticed that the storage room door had a lock on it.

"Sure, I guess." Nick eyed her with some suspicion. "What do you need my time for?"

"Just a question or two. Have you heard what happened?" Samantha raised an eyebrow.

"Yes, I heard." Nick lowered his voice. "It's getting around the ship even if the company would prefer it didn't."

"I see." Samantha nodded. "Well, I was wondering if you remembered seeing Carson around anywhere last night. I'm trying to piece together his last moments, but there weren't a lot of people around at the time of night that he was killed."

"I still can't believe that he was murdered." Nick sighed, then took a deep breath. "Generally, the ship is a safe place to be, but now, I'm sure all of the passengers will be very upset. I'm not sure what to tell them. But as for Carson, no I didn't see him last night. Not after I left him on the deck. He was with Annabella then. I figured he would be fine. Until—" He paused.

"Until what?"

Nick glanced away. "I'm sure it was nothing."

"What do you mean, what was nothing?" Samantha narrowed her eyes.

"I know that Annabella was supposed to stay with Carson all the time, but I also know that she wasn't with him all night. I saw Annabella in the bar. I even waved to her." Nick frowned. "She wasn't alone. She was with a man, his name is Karl."

"Karl?" Samantha raised an eyebrow. "Did she seem to know him well?"

"No, I doubt it." Nick lowered his voice. "I think she probably wanted to know him better, though. The way she was flirting with him."

"Flirting?" Samantha narrowed her eyes. "Are you sure about that?"

"Sure, I'm sure. I noticed because Karl's wife wasn't far away. She'd just gone out to the deck to have a cigarette. I was a little concerned that if she came back in and saw Annabella talking to Karl the way she was, there might be a fight." Nick frowned. "It happens on these cruises more often than you'd think, and it's important to end it as quickly as possible so that it doesn't get out of hand."

"Did Karl's wife come back in?" Samantha typed a note into her phone.

"No, she didn't. Not that I saw. I had to go

check on something on the deck, so I don't know what happened after that."

"And you didn't see Carson after that?" Samantha leaned against the wall as she looked him over. He appeared to be in his twenties, if that. "You didn't go looking for a tip?"

"No, I didn't see him. I was occupied with other things." Nick cleared his throat.

"So, even though you knew he should be with Annabella, you didn't go looking for him?" Samantha noticed the twitch in his right eye.

"No, I just assumed he was in his cabin. It isn't my job to keep tabs on him, it's Annabella's job." Nick frowned. "I didn't have any idea that he could be in trouble."

"Did he mention anything to you about any trouble he had with any of the passengers on board?" Samantha looked back down at her phone.

"No, he didn't. He didn't speak to me much other than to ask me for things." Nick rubbed his hand along his hip and then turned away from her. "There was something a little strange that I noticed, though."

"What was that?" Samantha noticed that he avoided her eyes, even when she walked around him and attempted to make eye contact.

"There was this guy taking photos of them. He went everywhere they went. At least that's what it seemed like to me. I didn't think much about it at first, it's a crowded ship. But then I noticed he was everywhere we were. He's a passenger on the ship. James Barker. I asked one of the other stewards, just to make sure that he wasn't a stowaway or something. I thought maybe he was a reporter."

"What gave you the impression that he might be?" Samantha added his name to the note on her phone.

"Just that he had this look about him. Like he didn't want to be seen. You know how sketchy people can be." Nick nodded. "And of course, the fact that he kept taking photos of them."

"Thanks for sharing that with me, Nick. I appreciate it. What does he look like?" Samantha asked.

"He's about thirty, I guess. Quite big and tall, with long, black hair tied in a ponytail." Nick nodded.

"Do you know what cabin he's in?" Samantha asked.

"No, I don't, sorry." Nick shook his head.

"Thanks Nick. You were one of the last people

to see Carson alive." Samantha's voice softened. "I'm sure that all of this came as a shock to you."

"I didn't expect it, that's for sure. I've heard stories before of murders happening on cruise ships, but I never expected it to be this one." Nick looked into her eyes. "So, why don't you ask me what you really want to know?"

"I'm not sure what you mean." Samantha straightened her shoulders and waited for further explanation.

"I'm not stupid. I know why you're here, asking me questions." Nick glared at her. "You think I had something to do with his death. I don't know who you are to him. Or anything about you. But I can see it in your eyes, the accusation."

"Nick, I just wanted to know what you might have seen. I didn't know Carson at all. But I do know that no one deserves to be murdered. And, I'd like to see his murderer caught." Samantha didn't shy back from his glare, instead she held his gaze. "And I don't intend to get off this ship until I do."

"He was a nice old guy. He tipped really well. Why would I want to do anything to hurt him?" Nick rubbed his hands together.

"I'm sure you didn't do anything to hurt him." Samantha met his eyes. "If you think of anything else unusual about that night, please be sure to let me know."

"You, or Blake?" Nick chuckled as he shook his head. "What are you thinking? This isn't a murder mystery cruise, you know? This is real life."

"I know that." Samantha spoke sternly. "My friends and I are just offering some assistance until the proper investigators are able to arrive."

"Right." Nick glared at her. "Just keep your little investigation, out of my business." He turned and stalked away.

"A bit defensive, isn't he?" Samantha raised an eyebrow as she watched him walk away. She looked down at the note on her phone. The name Karl stared up at her. Annabella claimed she wasn't in a relationship with Carson. Maybe she was looking for her next opportunity for a free ride. She hated to think it, but she couldn't deny the possibility. If Annabella was focused on flirting with Karl, maybe she had a plan. Did she want to take him from his wife? She had the looks to do it, that was for sure. But was Karl interested in cheating on, or leaving his wife?

As Samantha headed back towards Eddy's cabin, her mind swirled with the possibilities. It occurred to her that maybe Nick had been purposefully evasive about the reason he had to leave the bar. Maybe there was more the young man needed to keep hidden.

A knock on the door summoned Eddy to his feet. He pulled it open to find Samantha on the other side.

"Any news?" She met his eyes.

"Nothing solid, unfortunately. I did find out that Bobby has a bit of a temper, and that it seems he worships money. But that doesn't make him a murderer." Eddy stepped aside to let her in. "What about you?"

"I did manage to track down Nick, but he didn't have much to say either, other than he wanted me to leave him alone. However, he did tell me that a man named James Barker was following the couple taking photos of them. He didn't know what cabin he is in, though."

"I think I met a man with that name at the hotel bar before we set sail." Eddy nodded. "I'll see if Blake will tell me what cabin he's in."

"Hopefully, he will. Nick also said that Annabella was flirting with a man in the bar when

Carson was on the deck. Maybe when he was being murdered. I haven't been able to get more information about him yet, but according to Nick, he is married." Samantha sat down on the edge of the bunk bed. "I think it might be possible that she was looking to move in on him. But I don't know that for sure."

"At least we have some idea about the people that were around Carson. Have you seen Jo?" Eddy sat down in the wooden chair beside the small table.

"She said she was going to see what she could find out, but I haven't heard from her since." Samantha glanced at her phone. "No texts. I'll send her one to check in."

As she did, her phone began to ring with a video call.

"It's Walt." She smiled as she answered the phone. "Hi Walt. Did you find out anything about Bobby?"

"I did find something interesting." Walt smiled at Samantha, then nodded to Eddy as Samantha set the phone up on the table. "It looks like Bobby had made quite a few investments with Carson, and not all of them went well."

"That might explain why he had such a problem with Carson." Samantha tapped her fingers on the edge of the bunk bed. "Do you think it's possible that he knew Carson was going to be on the ship? Maybe he planned this whole thing?"

"I'm not sure. Honestly, Bobby has more money than he needs. The failed investments probably didn't hurt him too much. I'm not sure that he would be homicidal over it." Walt smoothed his hair back.

"You haven't met Bobby." Eddy chuckled. "I don't think he takes anything more seriously in life than his money. Even losing a little bit might have set him off, I think."

"Interesting. Well, from what I can tell Bobby's financial activity is on the up and up, there's no criminal history there, no reports of violence. I still think it would be a pretty big leap for him to kill someone."

"Maybe so." Eddy nodded. "Did you find out anything else?"

"Actually, since money is always a big motivator, I decided to look into who would potentially inherit Carson's fortune. He didn't have any children or living siblings. Even though he didn't have any children, he did have three nephews, they are brothers. They are the only relatives I can find. Caleb, Adam, and Drew. I need to still find out if

Carson had a will, and if he did who the beneficiaries are." Walt leaned closer to the camera. "Of course, I tried to check to see if I could find out if any of the nephews had a ticket for the ship, but that information isn't easy to ascertain."

"I can ask Blake to check the passenger manifest." Eddy sat forward in his chair. "I'm not sure if he will though."

"I might be able to track their recent locations and find out if any of them is missing in action." Samantha narrowed her eyes. "If they are, it might be because they are on the ship."

"That's a good idea." Eddy looked over at her. "But wouldn't Carson recognize them?"

"Probably, but maybe he doesn't know them. I guess it would depend on how involved he was with them. Maybe he didn't have anything to do with them. He might not know them from a stranger." Samantha sighed as she sat back on the bunk bed. "Some people have no relationship with their family."

"That's true. I can get Chris to run a background check on the nephews, see if they have any history of violence or connections with anyone who might have a history of it." Eddy pulled out his phone and sent a text to his friend Chris in the police department. "It may take a little time though, and with this storm coming in we might lose reception."

"About that storm." Walt spoke in a louder voice. "It's looking pretty nasty, Eddy. Where's Jo? I couldn't reach her." He craned his neck as he looked into the camera. "Isn't she there with you?"

"No, she went off to investigate something." Samantha checked for a notification of a text on her phone. "I haven't heard from her yet."

"Well, when you do make sure that the three of you hunker down. Hopefully, they can change course, but if not, I think the storm will be in your area by about tomorrow morning. I'll let you know if that changes. If there's anything else I can do from here, let me know." Walt ended the call.

Samantha picked up her phone and dialed Jo's number.

"Maybe she's on deck. The reception might be bad in this area. If the storm is getting closer it's possible that the phones are already being affected, she might not even be getting your texts or calls." Eddy walked towards the cabin door.

"All right, I'm right behind you." Samantha followed after him.

As they emerged on the deck, a strong wave slammed into the side of the ship. Samantha instinctively grabbed the railing to steady herself even though the ship didn't move. She noticed the huge waves surrounding them.

"I don't see her anywhere." She surveyed the portion of the deck that she could see. "She could be anywhere."

"She could be, but I'm sure she'll turn up." Eddy looked out at the sky. "It won't be long before that storm gets here. I can feel it in my hip, and my back." He ran his hand along the curve of his hip. "It's going to be a strong one."

"Do you think we should be concerned?" Samantha met his eyes as he looked back at her.

"I doubt it, but I can't say for sure. They say the way ships are built nowadays means you can barely feel the waves. Maybe they can avoid the storm. I know that the crew is trained to handle this, so we will be in good hands." Eddy placed his hand against her shoulder. "Does that make you feel better?"

"Actually, no." Samantha gritted her teeth. She dialed Jo's number again. She wasn't sure if she was more worried about the storm that approached, or the killer on the loose on the ship.

"Karl, get back here!" A woman's voice tore across the deck.

Samantha looked up as she recognized the name.

A man hurried past her, with a woman close on his heels.

"That's him." Samantha hurried to catch up with him.

"That's who?" Eddy stared after her.

"I'll update you soon. See if you can find Jo." Samantha waved to Eddy. She followed Karl and his quite angry wife into the nearest restaurant. Within seconds they were seated. Samantha hung back and watched the pair for a few minutes.

"Connie, it's not what you think." Karl rubbed his hand across his eyes. "It's just that it surprised me to hear of the guy dying. Is that so wrong?"

"It wouldn't be if that was what was really going on. I know you better than that, Karl. You don't get upset about people dying unless you feel a personal connection to them. So stop lying to me, and start telling the truth." Connie leaned forward to look into his eyes.

Samantha saw her chance and decided to move in. If she was going to find out anything about Karl, she would have to insert herself into the conversation. As she started towards them, she caught sight of Jo out of the corner of her eye. She walked beside a man who wore a chef's uniform.

"If you find out anything, please tell me." Jo smiled.

"Sure, I will." The chef's smile grew wider.

"Jo?" Samantha walked over to her. "I've been calling you and texting you."

"I know you have, it's been very annoying." Jo rolled her eyes. "I can't exactly get information from people if you are calling and texting me the whole time."

"I just wanted to make sure that you were okay." Samantha frowned.

"I'm sorry, I didn't mean to worry you." Jo sighed and brushed her long, dark hair back over her shoulders.

"Did you find out anything from the crew?" Samantha tipped her head towards the chef. "I assume that's who you were talking to?"

Jo gave a quick glance over her shoulder, then nodded.

"I thought if I could get some information from the staff, they might know more about what happened. But so far, I've come up empty-handed. I'm going to go see if Eddy or Walt have found out anything."

"Good idea. I have my eye on someone to speak with right now." Samantha watched as the couple handed over their menus to the waitress. "I'll check in with you two later."

Samantha didn't even notice as Jo walked away, her focus settled on the two who still squabbled with each other. She snapped a photo of them on her phone so she could send it to Walt, Eddy and Jo so that they would know what the couple looked like. After a few deep breaths she walked over to their table. This was something she had to do, if she was going to find out what happened to Carson. But confronting strangers, never worked out well for her. She hoped that this would be the one time that things would go smoothly. Samantha walked over to their table, with her heart pounding.

CHAPTER 8

"Karl, and Connie, right?" Samantha looked down at him, then at the woman beside him.

"Yes, that's us." Karl watched her sit down at their table across from them. "Do we know you?"

"No, not at all." Samantha gestured to the waitress. "Could I please have a cup of tea."

"Uh, excuse me?" Connie gazed at her. "Are you lost maybe? Do you have someone you're supposed to be sitting with?"

"No, I'm not lost. I'm sorry, it was rude of me to just sit down at your table, but I am dying for a cup of tea, and I need to talk with both of you, so I figured, two birds with one stone, right?" Samantha smiled as she looked between them. "You don't mind, do you?"

"Actually, we were hoping to share our meal alone." Karl narrowed his eyes. "What do you want to talk to us about?"

"I'm sure you've heard the rumors floating around the ship." Samantha took a deep breath, then folded her hands in front of her. "I know it has to be so disturbing to think that someone passed away on board this ship."

"Passed away?" Karl lowered his voice. "We heard that the man was murdered."

"Yes, that's true. At least, that's what I've heard as well. I noticed the man on the ship before he was killed. He was hard to miss with that hat and that scarf. Now, I feel so awful that he's gone. Did you know him?" Samantha looked into his eyes.

"No, not really." Karl shook his head.

"You never saw him?" Samantha raised an eyebrow.

"Yes, of course I saw him. But it wasn't as if we shared dinner together or something." Karl shrugged.

"What is this all about?" Connie narrowed her eyes.

"Not another word, Connie." Karl turned his

gaze from Connie to Samantha and stared straight at her. "I'd like you to leave our table, now."

"Oh yes, sure I can do that." Samantha tried to ignore the sweat that gathered on her forehead. "I'm sorry to have disturbed you." She stood up from the table, then paused long enough to look back at them. "I suppose you might have known his companion Annabella?" She watched Karl's reaction closely. Though his lips did tighten, his eyes remained settled in a glare. It was hard to tell if he even recognized the name.

"Annabella?" Connie growled. "I knew it! I knew you had a thing for her when I caught you staring at her yesterday! Did you take her back to our cabin?"

"Nothing happened!" Karl held his hands up in surrender. "Nothing, I swear."

"Sure, just like nothing happened on the last cruise that we went on." Connie scowled.

As the two continued to squabble, Samantha walked away from the restaurant. She headed instead to the one place she believed she might be able to get some answers. When she knocked on Annabella's door, she wasn't sure if the woman would open it. A few seconds later the door swung open.

"Samantha?" Annabella blinked.

"Annabella, can I come in?" Samantha felt frustration rush through her. She had come to Annabella's defense, and now it seemed as if all of the evidence pointed in her direction.

"Sure." Annabella led her into the spacious cabin. "I haven't ventured outside. I'm sure the ship is buzzing with the news. I don't want to get caught up in it. I don't want people looking at me strangely." She dabbed at her puffy, red eyes with a well-used tissue.

"Annabella, it's time you told me the truth." Samantha took the woman's hand and looked into her eyes. "Were you and Carson together? In a real relationship?"

"We've already talked about this." Annabella waved her hand to dismiss the conversation.

"I don't think you've told me the truth about it, that's not the same thing." Samantha frowned. "Do you really want me to let Blake know about that kiss so that he and the rest of the security team can interview you and work out you've been hiding things about your relationship. I'm sure they will appreciate hearing the truth as well."

"No, don't do that." Annabella cringed.

"Then tell me. Were you and Carson in a relationship?" Samantha gazed at her.

"Yes, all right?" Annabella sighed as she looked into Samantha's eyes. "We were together. Actually, we weren't just together." She frowned as she looked down at her hands. "We were married."

"Married?" Samantha took a sharp breath. "What do you mean?"

"I mean, the cruise was supposed to be our honeymoon. We got married right before we boarded the ship." Annabella rolled her eyes and leaned back. "It was all Carson's idea. We were just supposed to take a romantic trip together, somewhere away from prying eyes, away from judgment. But when we arrived at the hotel the day before, he told me he'd planned a ceremony for us, and that he wanted to get married before we left."

"And you agreed?" Samantha's heart began to pound. If what Annabella said was true, then with Carson's death, it was possible that she would become a very wealthy woman. It seemed a bit too convenient that the two would get married right before Carson was killed.

"Yes, of course I did." Annabella wiped at her eyes. "Carson had this way about him. It was like he created this new world around us. Nothing else mattered but the two of us, and the way we felt about each other. When I was inside that bubble with him, I felt like we could do anything. Our age difference didn't matter, his family didn't matter, my family didn't matter. It was just us, on this crazy adventure, and—" She paused and looked down at her hands again. "And we were very much in love." She looked up suddenly. "Have you ever had that connection with someone? Do you know what I mean?"

"I can't say that I do." Samantha gazed back at her. "But I understand what you're saying. Your connection was powerful."

"It was more like, his connection to me. He never doubted it, not once. I did." Annabella cleared her throat. "I hate to admit it now, but I did. When I first realized I was falling for Carson, I thought I had lost my mind. The first time we kissed, I questioned my own motives. I wondered if I was dazzled by his wealth, if I was drawn in by his strong presence. He just seemed so powerful." She took a breath. "But the more I fought it, the more intense it became, and the more certain I finally was when he asked me to join him in the ceremony. I'd never felt that way about anyone before." She gulped back a sob. "And I'm sure I never will again."

"I'm so sorry for your loss, Annabella. It sounds like the two of you had an amazing relationship. You were so in love." Samantha stroked the back of Annabella's hand. "I don't mean to upset you. I do believe that you had a close relationship with Carson. But someone observed you flirting pretty heavily with another man in the bar last night." She braced herself for the woman's fury.

"Who told you that?" Annabella's eyes narrowed. Her muscles tensed, but she didn't move any closer to Samantha.

"It doesn't matter. I know you went to the bar after you left Carson on the deck. You met someone who interested you in the bar, didn't you?" Samantha shifted closer to Annabella. It was hard for her to form the words. She didn't want to cause the woman any more suffering than she had to, but Eddy was right, the questions needed to be asked.

"I went there alone. Just to have a drink." Annabella clasped her hands together and lowered her voice. "I met someone while I was there."

"Someone's husband?" Samantha locked her eyes to Annabella's. She wanted to see the woman's reaction to the accusation.

"What?" Annabella blinked, then nodded. "All right, yes. But I was just friendly with him."

"Just friendly." Samantha noticed the way Annabella shifted in her seat and avoided eye contact.

"Yes, I spoke to him for a bit. He started flirting with me, so I just left. I wanted to go back to Carson."

"I'm still confused about the two of you being married." Samantha glanced at Annabella's folded hands. "You're not wearing any ring."

"That's because we intended to keep the marriage a secret, at least for the moment. I knew that most people wouldn't approve." Annabella pursed her lips and glanced away. "People can he horrible."

"They can be cruel." Samantha nodded.

"Someone was cruel enough to kill an innocent old man that never caused any harm to anyone. The truth is, he might have only had a few years left. He had recently decided that he didn't care what the doctors said, he was going to live his life the way he pleased, and that included taking up drinking again and following a terrible diet. I tried to convince him to seek healthier options, but he said he wanted his last few years on earth to be filled with good food, good memories, and good friends." Annabella shrugged. "Once Carson had an idea in his mind it was pretty impossible to talk him out of it. So, I guess, in a way, I was just going along for the ride."

"I understand that." Samantha wondered if Annabella had ulterior motives for marrying Carson, but if she sympathized with the woman, she might get more information out of her.

"People can judge me all they want, it doesn't bother me." Annabella crossed her arms as she stared at Samantha. "I will be investigated from top to bottom, because I am the thirty-two year old that married a man more than twice my age, a wealthy man to boot. I will be the main suspect in his death, because yes, I will benefit from it. Or maybe I won't. I have no idea. Carson and I got married in a brief ceremony before we boarded this ship. We didn't discuss any other details about what that meant. For all I know he could have planned to leave his fortune to his nephews. In fact, as much as he loved them, I'm sure he did." Annabella sank back down, and closed her eyes as fresh tears rushed past. "But no one will ever look at me and offer me genuine sympathy for my loss." She opened her eyes again, tears welled up in them, and she gazed at Samantha. "Maybe it would have been better if I never loved Carson so much, then I would never have to know this kind of pain. Maybe you are the lucky one, to never have loved, than to have loved and lost. Either way, I don't want you anywhere near me again. Do you understand? I can see that you are pretending to be my friend while you judge me as a possible murderer." She pointed to the door. "Please go, or I will call security myself."

"I'll go." Samantha stood up, though her legs threatened not to hold her. The woman's tirade had affected her. Was Annabella right? Was she judging her based on her own lack of experience with the kind of love she described? The possibility left her unsettled as she stepped out the door. A second later, her thoughts cleared, and she realized that Annabella had a far stronger motive now that she knew that she and Carson were married. No matter what stories she told, or what emotions she insisted on displaying, she would likely now be a very wealthy woman, due to Carson's death.

As Samantha headed for Eddy's cabin, she pushed down that rattled feeling within her and focused instead on the possibility that Annabella had everything to do with her husband's murder. Perhaps her flirting with Karl had led to something else. Maybe she and the couple decided to work together to make the trio rich beyond any of their dreams. If that was the case it would explain why Karl didn't want Connie to say another word to Samantha. She shivered at the thought. Was this an organized hit? Annabella might not have been able to pull off the murder on her own, but she could have hired someone to help her.

CHAPTER 9

Walt sat back in his chair and stared at the computer screen. He breathed through a bout of anxiety. The idea that Jo was off somewhere on that giant cruise ship investigating a murder, made him want one of two things. Either, for her to be at the hotel with him, or him to be on the ship with her. However, neither was a possibility. He could only focus on finding out what happened to Carson, so that hopefully the remainder of their cruise could be enjoyable. Though, he wasn't sure that any of them would be able to relax and enjoy a sunny vacation after a passenger had been killed on the ship.

Walt pushed the thoughts from his mind and focused instead on finding out as much information as he could about Carson's nephews. They were the only family he knew of that Carson had. Samantha had found that all three brothers could be accounted for. Although she hadn't managed to speak to any of them, she had ascertained that they were either at home or traveling for work. From what she could tell none of them were on the cruise ship. Chris had found no signs of criminal history in their past. But Walt wanted to see what he could find out about them.

"All right boys, let's see who you are and how you are involved with your rich uncle." Walt stretched his fingers, then began to type on the keyboard. Within minutes he had the social media accounts of all three brothers up on his screen. He could see that each of the siblings was in a transition period of their lives. The oldest had just switched careers, the youngest had just gotten married, and the middle boy had welcomed his first child. None of the comments on any of the posts appeared to have come from Carson. That wasn't entirely surprising. It was possible that Carson wasn't active on social media. What did surprise him was the fact that several of the likes and comments did come from Annabella. In fact, she commented as frequently as other friends and relatives. Whether or not the boys were involved with their uncle, Annabella had certainly made her presence known in their lives. Considering that she was not much older than the oldest nephew, he guessed that they might have hit it off by sharing things they had in common.

Walt shifted gears and sorted through Annabella's profile. She didn't post much. Though he looked for pictures of Annabella with Carson he didn't find any. She did mention that she loved her job and felt fulfilled by it. She also didn't post any pictures of herself with a boyfriend or show any interest in being involved in a relationship. He frowned as he switched back to the information on the nephews. As these were probably the people who were closest to Carson, he was certain that there had to be some kind of information available for him to find.

As Walt pored over the posts, he did catch a few details about the nephews' lives that he overlooked the first time. Though the middle nephew, Drew, portrayed a happy marriage, he noticed some frayed edges in some of the comments his wife made or didn't make. The youngest, Adam, who had just tied the knot appeared blissfully happy, but he also mentioned car trouble and housing woes. The oldest of the three, Caleb, complained about his old boss holding him back from the career that he deserved. He had only been in his new position for a few weeks. Walt documented the information he thought would be valuable, then collected recent photographs of each nephew. They all looked very similar and they looked familiar to him, but he couldn't place them.

Walt wanted to find out who gained from Carson being dead. After doing some research, he managed to find the name of Carson's lawyer. He was pleasantly surprised to see that he had previous dealings with him when he worked as an accountant. After a long conversation catching up, Walt found out that as far as the lawyer knew Carson didn't have a will. He had pushed him to get one, but he said he didn't need it. It appeared as if now that Annabella was married to Carson, she would inherit everything.

"That would certainly give her a motive." Walt sat back in his chair. He needed to share the information with his friends.

"Hello?" Jo smiled into the phone as the call connected.

"Jo, good to see you." Walt smiled in return.

"I think I should have stayed on land with you."

Jo sighed as she looked off to the right. "Eddy, Samantha, it's Walt with an update."

"It is quite an update." Walt watched his two other friends come into view.

"What is it, Walt?" Eddy asked.

Walt explained what he had found out about the fact that Carson didn't have a will.

"That's very interesting." Samantha sighed.

"It certainly gives Annabella a stronger motive, that's for sure." Eddy's eyes widened.

"I looked into the three nephews, but I didn't find much." Walt shook his head. "I couldn't find anything in relation to Carson and his nephews online. However, there were posts by Annabella on the nephews' social media profiles. Carson is a bit of a ghost when it comes to social media."

"You're right." Samantha rolled her eyes. "I couldn't find much about him, except what was on Annabella's profile."

"Annabella's profile? I didn't see anything on it about Carson." Walt frowned. "Are you sure you did?"

"Yes, her entire feed is all pictures of Carson, including some of her and Carson." Samantha raised an eyebrow. "I'm not sure how you missed it."

"What was the name on the account?" Walt tapped on his keyboard.

"Annabella Price." Samantha offered as she pulled out her own phone to check it.

"I have her listed as Annabella Lane Price." Walt looked back into the camera. "It sounds like she must have more than one account. With this account she commented on a lot of the nephews' posts."

"Interesting, I didn't see any posts on her account to the nephews. In fact, it's mostly all about Carson, she doesn't have too many personal connections herself." Samantha snapped her fingers. "I bet she keeps it separate since she's been hiding her relationship with Carson."

"Wise." Walt nodded. "But also conniving. I'll see what else I can find out about the brothers."

"You doing okay there, Walt?" Jo looked into the camera.

"I'd be doing better if there wasn't a massive storm headed your way." Walt looked into her eyes.

"Don't worry, we'll be fine." Jo winked at him, then ended the call.

Walt pursed his lips. If only it was that easy not to worry.

"I think our best lead at the moment is Nick.

Let's go have another chat with him. Blake did tell me that none of Carson's nephews were listed as passengers on the ship. But he hasn't got back to me about what cabin James Barker is in. But maybe Nick can tell me more about him. Maybe he has found out what cabin he is in." Eddy stood up and stretched his arms above his head. "Nick was following Carson around like a puppy dog. Maybe he noticed something else. Maybe now that he has had time to think about it, he remembers something else."

"That's a good idea." Samantha sighed as she stood up. "I guess my instincts really aren't what they used to be. Sorry for burning our bridges with Annabella."

"Don't be sorry." Jo smiled at her as she stood up as well. "Any information we got from her would likely be tainted. If it weren't for you, we might not have discovered that she and Carson had actually gotten married. That's an important piece of this puzzle."

"Yes, you're right about that." Samantha stepped out into the corridor. "Are you going to come with us to talk to Nick?"

"I think all three of us teaming up on him might be overkill." Jo shrugged as she watched them start down the corridor. "I have an idea of my own to follow up on."

"Good luck." Samantha called over her shoulder.

"Don't you think we should find out what that idea is?" Eddy glanced back at Jo before he continued down the corridor to catch up with Samantha.

"Jo is going to do as she pleases. Would you rather know what she is up to, or trust that she can handle it?" Samantha quirked an eyebrow.

"I'm not sure." Eddy frowned, then tipped his head towards the door at the end of the corridor. "If we take the stairs on the other side of the door, we should head down to the staff level. Blake gave me the layout of the ship when I spoke to him."

"It's good that he's willing to work with you on this." Samantha followed him towards the door.

"I'm not so sure that he's willing. But with help unable to get here, I'm all he's got." Eddy cleared his throat.

"Don't sell yourself short, Eddy, you know what a great investigator you are." Samantha gave him a light swat on the arm.

"Sure, sure." He rolled his eyes, then tipped his head towards the door that led to the stairs as it opened. A woman stepped out and walked towards them down the corridor. She wore a crimson shirt with the name of the cruise printed across the front. "Maybe she will know where Nick is."

"Excuse me." Samantha smiled at her as they crossed paths. "Would you know where a young man named Nick might be? He's a steward on the ship."

"Oh, he's up at La Siesta." The young woman smiled in return. "Some of the staff members are having a feast before the storm hits. If it gets really bad, we'll be in lockdown in our cabins, so better to fill up on the good stuff now." She waved to them as she walked away.

"La Siesta." Eddy looked at the steps he would have to climb to get to the next level. "I could sure use a nap."

"You're doing great, Eddy." Samantha patted his back. "You're not as old as you like to pretend you are."

"Who would ever want to pretend they are old?" Eddy scoffed and started up the steps.

"Maybe someone who finds it safer not to tell the truth, that he's just as spry and determined as he's ever been, and nothing about him has really changed." Samantha walked up the steps behind him. "I feel the same way, Eddy. I keep waiting for that moment when I am going to feel settled into my senior years, but it never happens." He looked over his shoulder at her. As his eyes locked to hers, Samantha smiled. "Don't worry, it'll be our secret."

"Has anyone ever told you that you have a very vivid imagination, Sam?" Eddy took the last step and moved onto the landing.

"Has anyone ever told you that your grumpy exterior does nothing to hide the handsome, caring, and strong man that you are on the inside?" Samantha smiled. When he looked at her, she found the stunned smile on his lips that she had hoped for. She winked at him, then continued along the deck in the direction of La Siesta. As the woman had indicated, the small Mexican restaurant was crowded with the ship's crew. Samantha looked through them and spotted Nick at a table by himself. He had an overflowing taco in his hands and was about to take a bite.

"Nick." Samantha paused beside his table.

"Uh-huh." Nick eyed her as he took a big bite of his taco.

"That looks good." Eddy grinned as he watched a bit of the meat tumble down onto Nick's plate.

"It is," Nick mumbled, then grabbed a napkin to

wipe up some of the sauce that dripped down his chin. "You again?" He looked at Samantha.

"Don't worry, we won't take up too much of your time." Samantha perched on the chair beside Nick. "How are you holding up? I know that you were taking great care of Carson. We just wanted to see if you remember anything else that might help find his murderer, now that you've had some time to think about it and the shock from the murder has died down a bit."

"I still can't believe it happened." Nick shook his head.

"Did you suspect that anything strange might be going on? Did Carson mention being afraid of anyone?" Samantha leaned a little closer to him and met his eyes. She was sure that he wouldn't be quick to volunteer any more information, but she sensed that Nick really was disturbed by what happened. Or perhaps by what he had done.

"Nothing like that, no. He was a funny guy, you know? He made everyone around him laugh. I can't imagine that anyone would have wanted to hurt him. But then, I didn't really know him that well." Nick took another messy bite of his taco.

"Someone certainly had it out for him." Eddy crossed his arms as he stood just to the right of

Nick's chair. With his demeanor he could turn on the intimidation factor in the blink of an eye. Whether or not Nick noticed it, he wasn't sure.

"Yeah, I guess." Nick sighed and stared down at the food on his plate. "Definitely a good tipper." He shifted in his chair. "I think he just liked having someone to talk to." He glanced up at Samantha. "He asked me not to mention it, but I've thought about it and I guess it doesn't matter now. He told me about his crazy wedding, right before he came on the cruise. He told me he was madly in love with Annabella and he was the happiest he'd ever been. That should count for something right?"

"Count for what?" Samantha tipped her head to the side.

"I mean, that he was so happy before he went. At least, that's something. I guess." Nick took another bite of his taco.

"Yes, I guess that is something." Samantha smiled some. "Did Annabella seem as happy as Carson?"

"I don't know, I didn't talk to her much." Nick wiped his mouth. "But like I said before, she was flirting with that married guy."

"Did you find out anything more about the couple?" Eddy asked.

"No nothing." Nick shook his head.

"We've been trying to find James Barker. The man you said was taking photos of Annabella and Carson," Samantha said. "Have you seen him again? Did you find out what cabin he's in?"

"No, I haven't. I have no idea, sorry. All I know is it's not one of mine." Nick took another bite.

"Enjoy your feast." Eddy smiled.

"Let's hope it's not our last. I think I'm going to have another one just in case." Nick filled his mouth with the rest of his taco.

As Samantha and Eddy walked away, Eddy looked over at her.

"Do you think we should be more concerned about this storm?" Eddy glanced back over his shoulder at the crew members that continued to dine.

"I'm more concerned about finding this James Barker."

CHAPTER 10

Jo navigated the corridors of the ship. As narrow as they were, they gave her a sense of confinement, one that made the hairs on the back of her neck stand up. The idea that perhaps they reminded her of her time in prison left her unsettled. She tucked that part of her life right back under thoughts of her current mission and hoped that it would stay there. She knew exactly who she wanted to speak to but tracking him down proved to be more difficult than she anticipated. There were several security offices on multiple floors. Her legs had begun to ache from the wandering and searching. But finally, it paid off when she saw the man she had been hunting.

"Excuse me, Blake?" Jo paused a few feet away

from the man. He nodded to the two guards he had been speaking to, then turned towards Jo.

"Yes? Can I help you?" Blake slid his hands into his pockets and stared at her.

"I'm a friend of Eddy's." Jo took a step closer to him.

"I know. I've seen you two together."

"I have some information that you might be interested in."

"You do?" Blake squinted at her as if attempting to figure out exactly how to take her.

"Yes, do you have a minute to discuss it?" Jo flipped her hair back over her shoulder and turned on the charm as she smiled. Despite the fact that she was easily twenty years older than Blake, she knew how to flirt with a man to get information she needed.

"Uh, sure." Blake shifted from one foot to the other, then directed her towards a small office off the corridor. "What kind of information do you have for me?"

"I'm not sure if it will help or not." Jo perched on the edge of the desk in the office, while Blake walked around to the side of it and picked up a pile of papers.

"Anything that you think might help, I want to

hear." Blake looked up from the papers and met her eyes. "Eddy has been a great help to me."

"I'm sure he has." Jo smiled as she held his gaze. "He's a very experienced and intelligent man. And very determined. I've come across some information that just might solve your murder."

"All right then, spill it." Blake set the papers back down and leaned his hands on the table. As he studied her, his body leaned forward enough to create only inches of space between them.

"Carson and Annabella got married shortly before they boarded the ship." Jo smiled as she looked at him. "She will most likely inherit his fortune, now that he's dead. I'd say that gives her plenty of motive."

"I agree." Blake took a slow breath, then straightened up. "You're sure about this? Where did you get the information from?"

Jo wasn't sure if it was the right thing to divulge the information, but she needed Annabella to be distracted, and this was the best way to make that happen.

"A reliable source." Jo tipped her head to the side. "I wouldn't be coming to you if I didn't believe it was true. I know you're a busy man with important things to do."

"I am." Blake cleared his throat, then straightened up. "I'll have a conversation with her."

"Good." Jo stepped away from the edge of the desk. "I wouldn't give her too long to make a plan. She might just find a way to cover up the truth."

"I won't give her any time at all. I'm going to bring her in for a conversation right now." Blake eyed her a moment longer. "Thanks for the information."

"Sure, anything to help this horrible situation get resolved. I'll let myself out." Jo walked to the door of the office, fully aware of his attention on her as she exited. Smiling to herself, she headed down the corridor back towards Annabella's cabin. She had hoped that Blake would speak to Annabella in his office not her cabin, and it looked as if that was exactly what he was going to do. She heard Blake step out of the office behind her. She listened as his footsteps followed after hers, until she passed by Annabella's cabin. She ducked around the corner of the corridor and listened as the two exchanged words.

"I need to speak with you in my office."

"Why? Has there been a development in the investigation?" Annabella's voice drifted around the corner to her.

"Possibly. I'd like to update you on what we've found so far, and perhaps get a little more information from you. Will you join me?"

"Sure."

Jo listened until the footsteps were too far away to hear. Then she peeked around the corner. She saw that there was no sign of the pair in the corridor, or anyone else for that matter. She was surprised that Annabella and Carson's cabins hadn't been cordoned off and Annabella told to move, since she knew that Eddy had suggested to Blake that this be done. Maybe Blake didn't want to upset Annabella further by asking her to move cabins? Maybe the ship was full?

Jo crept up to the door of Annabella's cabin and pulled out her lock-picking kit. She never left home without it, though she could easily use a paperclip or some other method to get the door unlocked if she had to. It was much easier when she could use her tools.

Before Jo could open the kit, she heard footsteps at the end of the corridor. She quickly put the kit away and walked away from the door. Jo saw someone at the end of the narrow corridor walking towards her. She walked towards him and as he walked past her she noticed that he was a tall, broad man with long, black hair tied in a ponytail.

Jo recognized that the man matched James Barker's description. He held a camera in his hand. She didn't want to let him get away, so she stepped boldly forward.

"Excuse me, James?" Jo asked.

"Yes." James frowned and looked at her. "Do I know you?"

"No sorry." Jo smiled sweetly. "I saw you taking photos and I was interested to know why?"

"Oh really?" James' expression grew tense. "Well, that really is none of your business."

"Why were you taking photos of Annabella and Carson?" Jo's voice hardened slightly.

"Oh." James' eyes narrowed. "You think I had something to do with Carson's murder?"

"No, I just wanted to find out who you are and what you were doing following Annabella and Carson around and taking photos of them?" Jo took a step forward and looked into his eyes.

"I guess it doesn't matter now." James shrugged. "I am doing an unauthorized biography on Carson." He smiled. "I'm a writer." He handed Jo a card. "I was gathering information for the biography."

"Can I see the photos you took?"

CRUISES CAN BE DEADLY

"No, I'm sorry, I don't share unedited pictures with anyone." James straightened his shoulders. "Especially given what's happened."

Jo thought about pushing the point, but she wanted to see if she could find out anything more from him before potentially alienating him.

"Did you see anyone acting strangely?" Jo asked.

"Here, come into my cabin." James gestured down the corridor. "I need to get this coffee off my shirt before it stains." He pointed to a brown stain on his shirt.

Jo hesitated. Did she want to go into the cabin of a potential murderer? She decided it was worth the risk. She wanted the information and she could take care of herself.

"Okay."

Jo followed after him and stepped into the cabin behind him. The cabin was large. Jo wondered if the three friends had landed up with the smallest two cabins on the ship.

James walked over to the table and placed his camera down next to a small camera bag on the table then went into the bathroom.

"I'll just be a minute." He called out.

As soon as James closed the bathroom door, Jo

didn't hesitate. She walked straight over to the small camera bag. She grabbed the cord in the camera bag and the digital camera and connected the camera to her phone. As she downloaded the pictures onto her phone, she noticed a few flick by. Many were of the past few days, including the night they all went to the restaurant at the hotel before the cruise set sail. She doubted they would hold any information, but it was worth getting her friends to look through them. Her heart pounded as she knew James could come out of the bathroom at any second.

As soon as the pictures had finished downloading, Jo pulled the cord free of her phone, tucked the cord back into the bag and put the camera back on the table, just as James opened the door.

"Sorry about that." James walked over to her with a clean shirt on. "What is it you want to know?"

"Can you tell me anything about Annabella and Carson?" Jo asked. "Were either of them acting strangely?"

"No, nothing out of the ordinary. But she had a fan, that's for sure." James smirked.

"A fan?" Jo narrowed her eyes. "What do you mean by that?"

"There was a guy following her around." James frowned as he leaned back against the wall.

"A guy?" Jo asked.

"I figured he had a crush. I mean Annabella is kind of hot. Maybe he didn't realize that Annabella and Carson were together. Anyway, he followed them everywhere."

"Do you know his name?"

"Yes, Todd Carpenter." James nodded. "I managed to get the receptionist at the hotel to tell me who he was."

"Can you tell me what he looks like?" Jo pulled out her phone.

"I don't know. Thirties I guess, maybe a little younger. Brown hair, pretty muscular. About my height. Glasses, he wore glasses." James squinted at Jo. "Why? Do you think he had something to do with what happened to Carson?"

"Not sure yet." Jo looked into his eyes. "Do you know what cabin he is staying in?"

"No idea." James shook his head. "I haven't seen him since Carson was murdered."

"Is there anything else you can tell me that might explain what happened to Carson?" Jo asked.

"No, sorry."

Jo wasn't ready to remove James from her

suspect list, but her instincts told her that he was innocent. He seemed honest and forthcoming with information. But was he just trying to divert suspicion from himself?

After warning James to be cautious as the killer might think he saw or caught something on the photos that might incriminate him, Jo left the cabin as her heart raced. She sent a text to Walt with the photographs she'd taken off James' camera. She knew it was risky to download the photos from his camera while he was in the bathroom, but she couldn't let the opportunity slip by.

Jo knew that it would be too risky to look in Annabella and Carson's cabins now. She was sure that Annabella would be finished with Blake soon, if she wasn't already.

Before Jo could get all the way down the corridor, Annabella passed her. If the woman recognized Jo, she didn't act as if she did. She wiped at her eyes with a tissue as she hurried in the direction of her cabin.

Jo held her breath until she was in the next corridor. She frowned as she glided past a group of tourists who had their eyes glued to the darkening sky. She didn't relax until she was up the flight of stairs to the deck.

CHAPTER 11

Walt couldn't shake the feeling that the nephews were familiar to him. He scanned through the pictures of them on social media, again. He focused on the eldest one, Caleb. He was sure he had seen him before.

"You, I know that face, and that red hair." Walt narrowed his eyes as he studied the picture on the monitor. "Caleb?" He sat back in his chair and tried to recall every moment since they arrived at the hotel. As he did, he churned through many faces. Walt's phone beeped with a text from Jo. It contained pictures of the hotel and aboard the cruise. He wondered where she had got them from. He skimmed through the pictures that Jo had sent.

His heart skipped a beat as he recognized one of the people in the photographs.

A tall, lanky man with shoulder length, red hair. In the hallway near the restaurant, at the hotel, before the others left on their cruise. He'd seen that face. It certainly seemed to him that the man in the photograph resembled the eldest nephew, Caleb. They had the same red hair. So, Caleb was at the hotel the night before the cruise? Walt realized he was right, he had seen Caleb before.

That would mean that Caleb was at the hotel at the same time as his uncle, but as he recalled he never approached or spoke to his uncle. Perhaps he had after they left? Or before? Or Walt just hadn't seen it?

"He was here at the hotel?" Walt's heart skipped a beat. "Is that really possible?" He looked at the photograph again. He had a strong attention to detail, but he knew that wasn't infallible. Maybe he just had the same hair color, maybe it wasn't the eldest nephew at all.

"It really could be him. It certainly looks like him." Walt shook his head in amazement. Were Caleb and his uncle traveling together? Was he there for the wedding? What were the chances that Caleb just happened to be at the hotel at the same time as his uncle if they hadn't arranged it? He decided to place a call to his friends on the ship. They needed to know about this development. Maybe they could help him sort it out. Despite the video call allowing him to connect with them face to face, it still was difficult to piece together what they might be up to or how they might be feeling. This was especially true in Jo's case, as she tended to be closed off to begin with. He picked up his phone to call her. As the phone rang, he again wondered if he should have joined them on the ship.

Jo had just opened the door to her cabin when her phone rang. She answered the call as her heart continued to pound.

"Are you okay?" Walt noticed the shortness of her breath.

"I'm fine."

"How did you get these pictures?"

"I happened to be invited into James Barker's cabin and I took them off his camera." Jo sighed. "That's not important now, Walt. What did you think of the pictures?"

"I think one of the people in a photograph at the restaurant at the hotel the night before the cruise left, is Caleb. Carson's eldest nephew. I just sent you some photos."

"Are you serious?" Jo frowned as she looked at the photos Walt sent. "Wow, it certainly looks like him."

"Have you seen him on the ship?" Walt asked.

"No." Jo shook her head. "But I could have missed him. This ship is huge. I think it's a long shot, but maybe he is still at the hotel. Maybe you can find out."

"I think you're right. Maybe he is." Walt took a deep breath. "Not about downloading the photographs off James' camera, that was risky, but you're right about possibly seeing if I can contact Caleb. It's important that we find out what he knows about all of this. I am going to see if I can find out if Caleb is still at the hotel first. If he isn't then I'll try to locate him and speak to him."

"I think it's strange that he was in the same place as his uncle, but Annabella made no mention of Caleb being there." Jo paused. "But maybe he was there for the wedding?"

"Maybe, that's what I thought. I'm going to see if he's still here. But I had considered that perhaps he slipped onto the ship." Walt shook his head. "But I think the fact that Annabella and Carson are married gave the nephews less motive to kill him."

"I agree, but it is still a lead that needs to be

followed. Maybe he has information on who might have killed Carson. I wonder who he is speaking to in the corridor." Jo's eyes narrowed. "Brown hair, glasses. That matches Todd Carpenter's description. But I'll see if I can find out more." She explained what she had found out about Todd from James.

"Are you being careful on the ship, Jo?" Walt counted the seconds before she responded. Two seconds meant truth, five seconds meant she was figuring out a lie that he would believe. Three, four—

"Of course," Jo replied. "Especially with this storm coming in. Everyone is being much more cautious."

"I'll keep track of that storm." Walt frowned. He was accustomed to Jo being evasive with him, but it only made him worry more. "Keep in mind if you get too close to the actual killer, you're going to be sitting ducks on that ship. You need to be extra careful."

"Ducks, is that supposed to be some kind of pun, Walt?" Jo laughed. "Don't worry, I am looking out for all of us. Pretty soon you'll be greeting us at the dock."

"I'll keep that in mind." Walt smiled. "It's still

possible that Caleb made his way onto the ship. So, keep an eye out."

"I will. I'm going to try to find Samantha and Eddy, now." Jo opened the cabin door and started to walk in the direction of Eddy's cabin.

Walt sighed as she ended the call. Although he understood her desire to protect his feelings, he wished she would be a little more comfortable telling him the truth.

"Jo, we've been looking for you." Samantha grabbed her by the arm and tugged her into Eddy's cabin.

"You are not going to believe what Walt and I just discovered." Jo held out her phone as she explained her encounter with James Barker. "This has a bunch of photographs on it from the night we were all at the restaurant at the hotel. From what Walt has found we are pretty sure that one of the photographs has Carson's eldest nephew, Caleb, in it." She flipped to the right picture.

"Carson's nephew was there at the hotel?" Eddy raised an eyebrow. "Maybe they were traveling together. If not, that's quite a coincidence."

"I really don't think it could be a coincidence that Caleb was at the hotel before the ship set sail." Samantha began to pace back and forth in the small space of the cabin. "If Walt is right and Caleb was at the hotel, and he got on the ship, then he could very well be the one behind the murder. Clearly, if his motive was money, and he didn't realize that Annabella and Carson got married and she would inherit everything, he had a reason to commit the murder."

"Or maybe he did know they were married." Eddy stroked his hand along his chin. "Annabella and Caleb are pretty close in age. Maybe they planned this whole thing together."

"That's an awful thought." Jo held up one hand. "Trust me I'm not one to judge, but to think that Carson would marry Annabella on a lovesick whim, only to be killed by her and his nephew. Ugh, it's just terrible."

"It is." Samantha nodded. "And, I'm not sure that I believe it. Maybe Caleb did find out about the wedding and was so angry because of it that he decided to try to stop it."

"Or maybe, he was just staying at the hotel." Eddy scratched the back of his neck. "We're not going to find out anything by standing around."

"I could ask Annabella, but I don't think she is ever going to speak to me again." Samantha's cheeks flushed as she recalled the way Annabella reacted to her.

"Walt thinks it looks just like him, and he was talking to this man." Jo held up the photo on her phone and pointed out the man in the corridor beside Caleb. They seemed to be trying to hide in the shadows.

"Thirties, brown hair, muscular, glasses." Eddy raised an eyebrow as he stared at the picture.

"That matches the description of Todd Carpenter." Samantha's eyes widened.

"That's what I thought." Jo nodded.

"Actually, I think I saw that man at the bar at the hotel. He sat next to James. Maybe I'm just remembering wrong." Eddy narrowed his eyes. "But that could be our stalker."

"Maybe." Samantha pulled out her phone and began to search the name Todd Carpenter. "If I can find his profile, we might be able to get a photograph of him." She frowned, then shook her head. "It's such a common name. Without knowing where he lives, I can't really narrow it down."

"Maybe we could get more information about him from the passenger manifest?" Eddy narrowed his eyes. "I might be able to get that information from Blake, if I play my cards right. Let me see if I can talk to him about it."

"You do that, and I'll see if I can hunt Todd down the old-fashioned way." Samantha opened the door to the cabin again. "We don't have time to wait around at this point. According to James, Todd Carpenter is a passenger on the ship. We can't know for certain that is the same person in the picture with Caleb, and even if we did, that doesn't mean that they are connected. But we have to find out why Todd Carpenter was following Carson or Annabella, either way."

"You're right." Jo nodded as she glanced over at Eddy. "Do you really think Blake will give you more information about Todd?"

"I can only hope so." Eddy frowned, then waved to Samantha as she slipped out the door. "I'll see if I can find him."

CHAPTER 12

Walt did his best to ignore his concern as he prepared to leave his hotel room. He had spent most of his time holed up in it, avoiding the myriad of germs and personalities that paraded past his door. But now he had a reason to step out into the chaos. He needed to find out what Caleb was up to. He needed to see if he was still at the hotel.

As Walt walked through the lobby, he gasped as he recognized a man close to the front desk. Could it really be so easy to find him? He had his phone to his ear, nearly buried in his red hair, and a briefcase clutched in one hand. It certainly looked like Caleb.

As Walt walked towards him, he didn't realize how slick the floor was. His shoe slid across the recently cleaned floor, and his slim frame was no match for gravity as it began to pull him down towards the ground. He flailed his arms out in an attempt to prevent himself from touching what he knew would still be a filthy surface teeming with germs. His hand struck something solid, and he grabbed it to steady himself.

"Hey, careful there!" Caleb grumbled as he tried to free his arm from Walt's grasp.

Walt looked up at him, stunned, and drew his hand back as he regained his balance.

"So sorry."

"Are you okay?" Caleb gazed at Walt.

Walt could only imagine the horrified expression on his face.

"I think so. Caleb, right? You're who I'm looking for. I want to talk to you about your uncle."

"My uncle? I don't know what you mean." Caleb frowned as he looked at Walt. "Are you sure that you're feeling okay?"

"I'm fine, thank you. I'm just wondering whether you realized that your uncle, Carson, was staying here at the hotel at the same time as you, a few days ago." Walt watched the man's expression for any sign of an attempt at deceit. "Were you traveling together? Were you here together?"

"Here at this hotel?" Caleb's eyes widened as he slowly shook his head. "I don't think he was here. Are you sure about that?"

"Yes, I'm sure. He was a passenger on a cruise that I was also supposed to be a passenger on. He stayed at this very hotel and in fact was in the same restaurant with you." Walt searched Caleb's eyes. "And you didn't notice?" He recalled just how packed the restaurant was. He didn't think it was impossible that Caleb hadn't seen his uncle.

"No, I didn't notice. If I had, I would have said something to him. I don't understand, what is all of this about? Why didn't you go on the cruise and what does any of this have to do with my uncle?" Caleb glanced over his shoulder in the direction of the front door of the hotel. "I really do have to be somewhere."

"I'm sorry. You haven't been contacted?" Walt swallowed hard as he realized that Caleb had no idea his uncle was dead. Or perhaps, he was doing a good job of hiding it.

"Contacted about what?" Caleb narrowed his eyes. "Is this some kind of sales scheme or something? I don't have time for this." He started towards the door.

"Wait." Walt caught him by the sleeve of his suit

jacket. He didn't often voluntarily touch people, but in that moment he couldn't allow Caleb to walk away. He drew his hand back, quickly, then took a step back as well. "I'm sorry to have to be the one to tell you this."

"Tell me what?" Caleb turned back towards Walt, his tone exasperated.

"Your uncle, he has passed away." Walt locked his eyes to Caleb's, prepared to endure whatever reaction the man had.

"You're lying!" Caleb raised his hand and took a step towards Walt as if he might strike him. "I don't know what your scam is, but this is really twisted!"

"It's not a scam." Walt took several steps back and winced. He had no interest in being struck. "I'm telling you the truth. The cruise company must not have been able to contact you. My friends are on the ship, they're the ones that told me about what happened. Carson was killed."

"Killed?" Caleb stumbled forward, his hand dropped back down to his side. "This can't be true." He pulled his phone from his pocket. "I have to call my brother."

"You should." Walt nodded as he watched the man fumble with his phone. He wasn't sure what he had hoped for. Perhaps less of a reaction, a coldness, or even celebration. But what he saw instead was genuine shock and grief. Maybe Caleb thought that he stood to inherit quite a bit of money, but at the moment he seemed far more concerned with the loss of his uncle than he was with his good fortune.

After Caleb hung up the phone, he looked back at Walt.

"You're telling the truth."

"Yes, I am." Walt shook his head. "I'm sorry, I wish it wasn't the case. I assumed that you already knew."

"Knew that an amazing man like my uncle is dead?" Caleb took a slow breath and released it at the same pace. "No, of course I didn't know. I wouldn't be here working if I did. My brother didn't tell me because he knew I would come home straight away when I found out, and I need to work." He rubbed his hand along his forehead and closed his eyes. "I can't believe he's gone."

"I'm very sorry for your loss." Walt clasped his hands together and watched the man. "Do you know if he'd been having any trouble with anyone lately?"

"I spoke with him just last week. We didn't talk often, but he told me about going on a cruise. I didn't know that he would be leaving from this hotel. Honestly, I was half-listening." Caleb sighed. "I always felt like I had more important things to do."

"Life can be so busy." Walt nodded as he moved a little closer to the man. He recalled Caleb's fist in the air, and didn't want to risk getting too close. "Did he mention anything else in the phone call? Anything that was troubling him?"

"Actually." Caleb's eyes widened. "Yes, now that you mention it. He did tell me that he was having some trouble with this guy named Bobby. That was part of the reason he was going on the cruise. He wanted to get away from Bobby's phone calls and threats. He said Bobby lost a lot of money on an investment and he wasn't taking it well."

"Bobby McPherson?" Walt raised an eyebrow.

"Yes, that's his name." Caleb eased himself down into an empty chair and gazed at the pattern on the floor tiles. "Someone did this to him?"

"Yes, I'm afraid so." Walt sat down in the chair beside him. He wondered what Caleb knew about Carson's relationship with Annabella. "Annabella is beside herself."

"Annabella?" Caleb blinked, then nodded. "Yes, I suppose she would be with him. She's been his assistant for some time. He was very dependent on her." He looked up at Walt again. "I wonder how this happened with her watching?"

"I believe Carson was alone when it happened."

"Wasn't that her job?" Caleb narrowed his eyes. "Not to leave him alone?" He shook his head with disgust and stalked off across the lobby.

Walt stared after him. Yes, it was Annabella's job. So, why had she left him alone?

CHAPTER 13

As far as Jo was concerned another person that they needed to cross off their suspect list was Bobby McPherson. He had motive, he had opportunity, and she imagined that he knew the ship better than anyone else who was on it.

Getting to him, would be rather difficult. She decided to use a ploy that had often worked for her before when she fished for a wealthy person to strike during her cat burglar days. As long as she appeared important, it was hard for most people in a position of power not to want her attention. She stopped in the cabin she shared with Samantha and took the time to smooth back her long, dark hair into a tight ponytail. Then she changed into the nicest clothes she'd brought with her, which consisted of black, pleated pants and a snug, sleeveless turtleneck. It wasn't anything she had planned to wear, but she brought a few extra pieces of clothing just in case. Samantha had said she should bring with an evening dress to wear to some of the dinners, but she was never one to dress too fancily. As Jo took a look in the mirror on the wall of the bathroom, she nodded to herself. With a bit of color and a lot more jewelry the look would have been more refined, but she didn't have those options. She headed back up to the deck and began to walk around as casually as she could.

"Excuse me?" Jo smiled as a woman paused beside her near the railing of the ship.

"Yes?" The woman met her eyes.

"Have you seen Bobby McPherson. I've been told he's someone that I should meet." Jo tilted her head to the side as her smile widened. "I've had a hard time hunting him down."

"I'm sorry, I don't know anyone by that name. Good luck finding him." The woman shivered as she looked out over the railing. "Good luck to us all, with this storm coming in."

"I'm sure it will pass quickly." Jo forced a bit of bounce into her voice. She wanted to believe the words she spoke, but she didn't. Between the sky and the churning of the waves around the ship she had begun to be more than a little concerned about the storm as well. She caught sight of a well-dressed man as he walked towards one of the restaurants along the interior of the ship. She had noticed him talking to Bobby shortly after he confronted Carson on the ship.

As Jo walked over to him, she was careful not to hurry. That was one thing she'd noticed about people who were important, they never seemed to have to hurry. She stood beside him. "Excuse me, maybe you could help me?"

"Help you?" He turned towards her, annoyed at first, as evidenced by the tight furrow of his eyebrows, but as he drank in the sight of her, his expression relaxed, and a smile spread across his lips. "Sure, what can I help you with?"

"I've been having some trouble finding someone I'd like to speak with. His name is Bobby McPherson. I think I saw you talking to him the other day." Jo smiled with confidence.

"Oh Bobby, sure." He nodded and shifted his stance so that he could lean a little closer to her. "Why are you looking for him?"

"We have a mutual friend, and she absolutely insisted that I spend some time with him when she heard that we would be on the same cruise." Jo rolled her eyes as she laughed. "I'm not sure why it's so important to her, but I promised her I would at least introduce myself, especially seeing as things are so unpredictable with the storm. I'd rather meet him sooner than later."

"Ah, I see." The man chuckled. "Someone is trying to play matchmaker perhaps?" He raised an eyebrow.

"I doubt that." Jo smiled sweetly. "I think we just have some mutual interests." She lifted one shoulder in a light shrug. "It's always good to have someone to chat with on a vacation like this."

"That's true. Last time I saw Bobby he was at the sports bar on the third level." He smiled. "He's probably still there. He was trying to catch the rest of a football game."

"Great, thanks so much." Jo smiled in return, then headed for the stairs. It would take some time to get to the third level. She hoped that Bobby would still be there when she arrived. As she headed down one of the corridors, she noticed Karl not far from a storage room. He leaned against the wall, which blocked his hands from view, but Jo recognized the subtle movements in his shoulders and arm. He was picking a lock. She was certain of it. She slowed down to take a closer look but noted the tension that rippled through his body. He likely sensed that he was being watched. She forced herself to continue to walk down the corridor. If she caught him in the act, she would never be able to find out what he was up to with that storage room.

When Jo made it to the third level, she discovered several restaurants she didn't even know were on the ship. They hadn't had much time to explore once Carson's body was found. The music that wafted out of the various restaurants tempted her senses, along with the delicious aromas. It was strange to be tantalized by festive environments, while the sky remained a stormy backdrop. She did her best to ignore a sensation of dread that rushed through her as she stepped into the sports bar. Within seconds she spotted Bobby. He wasn't far from the large television screen that hung along one wall. He slammed his fist down on the table he sat at, then cursed under his breath.

"Tough game?" Jo smiled as she paused beside him.

"I'm not sure I can even call it a game." Bobby's shoulders slumped. "It's just pathetic."

"Sorry to hear that." Jo shook her head. "I was

hoping that I'd be cheered up by coming in here, away from the storm."

"Sorry to disappoint you." Bobby tipped his head enough to look right into her eyes. "Who are you again?"

"My name is Jo." She offered her hand.

"Jo." He nodded. "I think I've seen you before."

"Probably. At the restaurant at the hotel, or on the ship since we left." Jo nodded. "I was told that you designed this ship, is that true?"

"Yes. I helped design it." Bobby sat forward.

"Do you think it will hold up okay in this storm?" Jo noticed beads of sweat scattered across his forehead.

"It'll be fine." Bobby nodded and held her gaze. "Nothing to worry about."

"I wish I could say the same for Carson. To lose someone you've worked with so closely, that must be very hard for you." Jo stared right back into his eyes.

"It's not easy, that's for sure. I had a problem with the man, but that doesn't mean I wished him ill." Bobby stood up from his chair.

"What kind of problem did you have?" Jo remained just as close to him.

"He wasn't good at his job." Bobby narrowed his eyes. "If you don't mind, I'd like to pass."

"I lost money with him, too. How much did you lose?" Jo crossed her arms. "Everyone's so upset about his death, but he nearly bankrupted me."

"You, too?" Bobby pursed his lips. After a quick glance around, he lowered his voice. "What he did to me was criminal, at least it should be. I won't be shedding a tear for him, that's for sure." He brushed past her, and out the door of the bar. She thought about following after him, but she doubted that she would get anything more from him. Bobby was a cold man, but he wasn't a stupid one. He'd only admitted to what everyone already knew, he'd had bad business dealings with Carson. That didn't make him a murderer. However, it also didn't cross him off Jo's list.

As Jo started back towards Eddy's cabin, she recalled Karl outside the storage room. She knew she wouldn't be able to rest until she had a look inside to see what he might have been looking for, or trying to hide. Clearly, something about that closet made it worth breaking into. With her thoughts focused on this she followed the same path that she'd taken.

Soon Jo found the storage room. A look up and

down the corridor revealed that she was alone for the moment. She didn't know how long that would last, so she decided to seize the opportunity. The lock gave way easily, she slipped inside and closed the door behind her. In the center of the darkness that surrounded her a thin, silver chain swung back and forth. It was just shiny enough to be seen through the murky shadows. She grabbed it, and pulled. An instant later the room flooded with garish white light. She took a sharp breath as she wondered if the light could be seen beneath the door to the storage room. It was possible that anyone in the corridor could have been alerted to her presence. She had to work quickly.

The shelves were lined with what she expected to see. Cleaning supplies, extra linens, there was even a stack of extra chairs in the back corner. Behind that stack of chairs was a small, zippered bag. She crouched down to have a closer look. It seemed to her that someone had taken the time to make sure that it wouldn't be easily found. If she hadn't been looking for something out of place, she never would have noticed it. As she tugged it free of the chairs it felt light, perhaps even empty. She unzipped the bag and discovered that it really was empty, aside from a few purple threads. She pulled them out of the bag and held them up into the light. The bright purple color made her eyes widen. Could they have been from Carson's scarf?

Footsteps outside the storage room made her heart skip a beat. She stuffed the bag back behind the chairs. It would be better if whoever put it there didn't know that it had been discovered. She held her breath as she listened to the footsteps in the corridor pass by the room. Only when she thought they were a safe distance away did she pull the chain on the light and bathe herself in darkness once more. She took a slow breath, then eased the door open.

The corridor was quiet and empty. She slipped out into it and pulled the door to the storage room closed behind her. If Carson was spotted on the security camera going back to his cabin, that meant that his clothes had to go somewhere. Suddenly it struck her that maybe Carson's body was missing some clothes, not because he was murdered in his cabin, but because whoever killed him had taken his clothes. It would be the perfect way to avoid being seen on the cameras that dotted the deck. Carson had been on deck, fully dressed, and he was seen walking back to his cabin. But what if it wasn't Carson that the camera captured? The thought made her freeze where she stood. All that was recorded on the video was a man in the same clothes that Carson wore. None of them had questioned that it was Carson, because no one else on the ship dressed exactly as he did. He even walked with an ivory cane. But if he had been killed in his cabin, someone would have had to move the body from the cabin to the lifeboat, and the chances of not being seen were slim to none. So, what if there was no body to move from the cabin to the lifeboat? What if Carson had never returned to his cabin?

Jo paused in front of Eddy's door and knocked on it. After a few seconds she realized that he likely wasn't inside. He had been on his own hunt to find Blake. Some voices drifted around the corner. She followed the sound of them around the corner and down the steps into the employees' quarters. At the bottom of the stairs she spotted Eddy and Samantha. Farther down the corridor she saw Blake and two security guards. For a split-second she wondered if they were looking for her because she had broken into the storage room.

CHAPTER 14

Samantha caught sight of Jo as she descended the last step and started in her direction. Before she could wave to her friend, Blake and two other security guards brushed past her mid-jog.

"Step aside please." Blake pushed past Jo as well, focused on getting to the next corridor.

"Where is he going so fast?" Eddy narrowed his eyes.

"Let's find out." Samantha caught his hand and tugged him down the corridor. "They're heading in the direction of the staff members' cabins."

"What's going on?" Jo frowned as she fell into step beside them.

"Not sure yet, but Blake is up to something."

Eddy followed after Blake, his steps swift and determined. "One of the guards just said something about going to Nick's cabin." He glanced back at the others.

"Blake must have found something out about him." Samantha quickened her pace to keep up with Eddy.

"We'll know soon enough." Eddy tipped his head towards the corridor. "Let's catch up before we miss something important."

Samantha and Jo matched Eddy's pace and the three of them managed to catch up with Blake and the other security guards, just as he pounded on Nick's door.

"What's this all about?" Eddy leaned against the wall with one hand. He sucked down a few hungry breaths, winded by the swift journey.

"The captain has requested that I take Nick into custody." Blake looked over at Eddy, then locked his eyes to Jo's, before he looked back at the door. "Open up, Nick. Right now."

"I don't think he's in there." Samantha spoke up, her eyes wide.

"What do you mean?" Blake turned towards her.

"We left him a short time ago in La Siesta, he was there with a few other crew members. I think he was going to be there a while longer." Samantha narrowed her eyes. "On what grounds are you taking him into custody?"

"On the grounds that one of my security guards recovered items missing from the victim's person in Nick's cabin." Blake crossed his arms as he looked between the three of them. "Did you tip him off that I was looking into him?"

"No, of course not." Eddy glowered at him. "We had no idea that you were on to him, so how could we? I thought we were sharing information?"

"That was the case, until your friend here clued me into something that you apparently didn't think was important enough to tell me about." Blake met Jo's eyes. "At least she was wise enough to share the information with me. The fact that you didn't tells me that you were never actually interested in helping me."

Eddy swung his gaze around to look at Jo. His eyes widened for an instant as Jo looked away from him, then he turned his focus back on Blake.

"I helped you in every way that I could. I gave you all of the relevant information that I found. Now, what does Nick have to do with any of this?" Eddy took a step closer to Blake.

"Excuse me?" Blake straightened his shoulders

and stared hard at Eddy. "Remember, you are nothing but a passenger here."

"What's going on?" Nick's voice drew all of their attention. He stood a few feet away, his cheeks flushed and his mouth half-open.

"Get him." Blake signaled to the two other security guards. "Nick, you're being detained until such time as you can be turned over to the proper authorities."

"Detained?" Nick stumbled back as the two security guards each grabbed one of his arms. "For what?"

"For the suspected murder of a passenger." Blake glared at him. "We found Carson's shoes, hat, scarf, jacket and cane in your room, along with his wallet."

"What?" Nick strained against the grasp of the security guards. "What are you talking about? That's not possible! I didn't do anything to Carson!"

"Take him." Blake nodded to the two security guards. "Make sure someone stays with him at all times. I don't want any mistakes. As soon as this storm passes, the investigators will arrive, and they will want to talk to him right away."

"Please Blake." Nick groaned as the two security guards began to drag him down the corridor. "I didn't do this. I didn't have any of that stuff. Why are you doing this to me?"

"It would be best to cooperate, Nick. You made a grave mistake, you'd better start thinking about how you can make a good impression on those investigators." Blake crossed his arms.

"Wait, are you saying you found all of that in Nick's cabin just now?" Eddy turned to face Blake. "If so, how didn't you know that he wasn't in his cabin?"

"I received a tip." Blake's cheek rippled as he clenched his jaw. "From someone who had been in his room. I had one of my guards check the room earlier, and when I received the pictures of the evidence they found, I took the information to the captain who authorized Nick's detention." He studied Eddy. "Things have to be done quickly on a ship. We can't have a murderer running around."

"He seems pretty upset." Jo frowned as she watched Nick disappear down another corridor. "He claims he had nothing to do with it."

"Did you expect him to confess?" Blake chuckled. He started to say more but before he could, the ship listed hard to the right. Blake stumbled into Samantha, who slammed into Eddy, who struck the wall. Jo hit the wall a few inches away from him.

"Ouch." She winced as pain shot through her shoulder. The ship settled in a more gradual movement which allowed all of them to get their footing.

"Wow, this is going to be bad. The storm is hitting earlier than predicted." Blake pulled out his radio and barked an order into it, then he holstered it again. "I need to get up top and see what's going on."

"Are you okay?" Eddy looked at Samantha.

"I think so." Samantha winced as she looked at him. "You're the one I ran into. Did I hurt you?"

"Not at all." Eddy smiled.

"Fibber." Samantha sighed as she noticed the strain in his expression.

"Let's get up top and see what this storm is doing." Eddy grabbed her hand, then followed after Blake.

As Jo matched their pace, she shook her head.

"I don't think it was Nick. I saw Karl breaking into a storage room, and when I let myself in, I found an empty bag with a few purple threads. I think it's the same color purple as Carson's scarf. It made me realize that the person that walked back to

Carson's cabin might not have been Carson at all." Jo kept her voice low enough that Blake couldn't hear. "I don't think Carson ever made it back to his cabin."

"You think someone else wore his clothes?" Samantha took a sharp breath. "That would certainly explain a lot. But if Carson's clothing and wallet were found in Nick's cabin then maybe he really did have something to do with it."

"Or maybe Karl planted the clothing in his cabin to make it look like he did." Jo raised an eyebrow. "If not Karl, maybe someone else. We can't be certain."

"No, but if the evidence is there, it's pretty safe to assume that Nick was involved somehow. Why would anyone go to all the trouble of framing him?" Samantha followed Eddy up the steps to the deck.

"To throw the scent off themselves. If they did that, it might mean that we're getting close." Eddy gripped the railing as a gust of wind threatened to knock him back. Hard rain pelted them from all directions. "It's harsh out here." Eddy shouted through the howl of the wind.

Another large wave crashed over the railing and sent a rush of water across the deck. It wasn't strong enough to knock Samantha off her feet, but she grabbed the railing just to make sure. Her heart began to race. It seemed to her that the storm was much stronger than they had expected, and it was only getting started.

"That's it!" Blake waved his hand through the air. "Emergency operations are in place! Everyone must return to their cabins and remain there until the ship is declared secure!" As he waved his hand again, a siren blared throughout the ship, followed by a recorded message that instructed every passenger and non-essential crew member to do the same thing. The few passengers on the deck scurried for the steps that led to the cabins. Eddy stood his ground as he glared at Blake.

"You're making a mistake by jumping at the first bit of evidence you've found. Nick might have had something to do with this, but you don't have enough evidence to declare him the killer. Have you even considered that someone else might have planted those items in his cabin?"

"I'm done with you telling me how to do my job." Blake glared back at him. "From now on, you're going to listen to me. Get to your cabin, and stay there, or I will have the captain detain you right alongside Nick. I need to get an update from the captain about this storm." He hesitated for a moment, then looked between Jo and Samantha. "Do as I say, or your lives could be at risk. Don't let this guy's ego talk you into doing something that you'll regret." He turned on his heel and stalked off.

"Maybe you want to tell me about what you told Blake?" Eddy pulled off his rain-soaked fedora and looked straight into Jo's eyes.

"It's a long story." Jo flashed him a smile.

"Good thing we have nothing but time." Eddy led the way down the steps to the cabins.

"Let's hole up together, Eddy." Samantha caught his hand as they reached the bottom of the steps. "We can figure out what's going on here, even if we can't leave the cabin."

"Sounds good to me." Eddy paused in front of their door. "As long as you don't mind sharing the space with my apparently quite large ego."

"Just get in here." Jo rolled her eyes as she unlocked the door. "I used Blake as a distraction so I could try to get into Annabella and Carson's cabins. That's how he found out about the fact that they were married. I needed him to have a reason to want to speak with her, to give me enough time to get into their cabins and take a look around. But then I saw James Barker and I didn't want to miss the opportunity to talk to him. I'm sorry, I know I should have checked with you first, but I thought it was a good piece of information to use so that I could get into their cabins. I thought I might find something important there."

"There's no time to talk about it now." Eddy frowned. "With Nick locked up, Blake has his main suspect, and he is going to be too preoccupied with this storm to do any further investigating."

"The problem is we haven't been able to find Todd." Samantha frowned. "I asked around while you were trying to find Blake to ask him, but I couldn't get any bites. If he is on the ship, either he is using a different name, or he has been keeping to himself."

"I'd say if I was going to be involved in a murder, I would definitely keep to myself." Jo sat down on the edge of the bunk bed. "But I'm not entirely ready to give up on the idea of Bobby being involved, and of course, there's still Annabella. From what we know she really had the most to gain from Carson's death."

"Yes, she did." Samantha sighed as she leaned back against the wall. "I want to solve Carson's murder as much as both of you, but are either of you the least bit worried about this storm?" She crouched down as the ship rocked hard.

"A little." Jo nodded, then narrowed her eyes. "More than a little."

"If it wasn't for Carson going missing, we wouldn't be in the middle of this mess." Eddy shook his head. "I'm sure that his killer wasn't counting on this. I doubt that whoever did this to Carson would risk trying to get off the ship at this point. Which means that the killer should still be on the ship. The problem is we have too many suspects and not enough evidence."

"All of the clothing and Carson's wallet being found in Nick's cabin is pretty good evidence." Samantha took a seat on the bunk bed beside Jo. "I agree with you, Eddy, that Blake is jumping to conclusions, but he has a lot of reasons to."

"I would probably agree with you as well if I hadn't seen Karl breaking into that storage room. If the clothes were stored there, and Karl knew that, doesn't that mean he could be the killer? The fact that now we believe Carson was killed on the deck means that it's much more possible for Karl to have killed him." Jo tugged the hair tie out of her hair and let it fall down around her shoulders. "But what motive would Karl have?"

"We know that Karl and Annabella were seen flirting in the bar." Samantha closed her eyes as the ship rocked again. "Maybe Annabella asked for his help. Maybe she offered to split her inheritance with him if he would be willing to kill Carson."

"It's possible." Jo nodded and raked her fingers through her hair. It was soaked from the rain and would take a long time to dry. "It's also possible that Annabella made the same arrangement with Nick, and that's why the clothing was in his cabin. Nick would know the ship well enough to get around unnoticed. Now that we know that Carson was probably killed on the deck it makes it more likely that either one of them committed the murder."

"I hadn't thought of that." Eddy nodded as he rubbed his chin. "That's definitely possible. But how would she know they wouldn't squeal. All of these theories lead back to Annabella."

"That isn't going to matter if we can't prove that she hired someone to kill Carson." Samantha gripped the side of the bed as the ship rocked from side to side. "Unless her accomplice admits to the crime, she could still get away with it."

"If Nick is the killer, that only leaves us with one possible witness." Jo pulled her phone from her pocket and flipped to the photograph of Annabella, Carson, and a stranger not far behind them. "Todd." She looked up at her two friends. "Maybe James was right, maybe Todd had a thing for Annabella. Maybe he wasn't the murderer, but he might have seen something that will help us figure out what happened to Carson."

"And if he did, he might be in danger." Samantha suddenly stood up. She steadied herself on Eddy's shoulder as the ship rocked again. "If the killer knows that Todd might have witnessed something, then this storm might be the perfect opportunity to get rid of him."

"You're not suggesting what I think you're suggesting, are you, Sam?" Eddy looked into her eyes.

"If we don't find out where Todd is, we might be dealing with two murders by the time the storm passes." Samantha shook her head as she made her way towards the cabin door. "I can't live with that. Neither of you have to come with me, but I'm going to find Todd. He should be in his cabin, like everyone else, which will make him easy for us to find, and easy for the killer to find, too."

"You're certainly not going out there." Eddy caught her by the arm. "Not alone."

"I'm right behind you." Jo sighed as she stood up. She tied her hair back up into a ponytail. There wasn't much chance of it ever getting dry.

CHAPTER 15

"If we have no idea what cabin Todd is in, how do you expect to find him?" Eddy trailed his hand along the wall of the corridor to give himself some sense of stability as the floor seemed to shift beneath them.

"That's where Jo comes in." Samantha grabbed Jo's hand as they rounded the corner and approached the steps that led to the deck.

"What?" Jo met Samantha's eyes.

"We need the passenger manifest. It should have all of the passengers listed along with their cabins. The captain should have a copy, and so should Blake. I'm guessing that Blake's copy is in his main office, which is one level above us." Samantha looked up at the ceiling. "He's going to be busy going through the ship to be sure that everyone is secured in their cabins. It's the perfect time to get the list." She gazed at her friend. "But only if you're willing to do it. I know that it might be too much to ask. I really do."

"It's not too much to ask." Jo frowned. "It's just risky. We have no idea where Blake actually is."

"I might be able to help with that." Eddy pulled out his phone. "I can give him a call. At least, if he picks up, I might be able to figure out where he is by the sounds in the background."

"If he picks up." Jo shook her head. "There's not much chance of that after the way he spoke to you. Besides, we can't risk him figuring out that we're not in our cabins either. I can do this, but I need you two to be lookouts."

"Absolutely." Eddy nodded and slid his phone back into his pocket.

"Whatever you need us to do, we will do it." Samantha then led the way up the steps, through the deck level, to the next cabin level. "It should be about halfway down the corridor." Samantha showed Jo an image on her phone. "I was able to get a list of security offices on the ship. This is the main one that I'm guessing he works out of most of the time. But like I said, it's his responsibility at the moment to ensure the passengers' safety, so he likely is out checking the corridors."

"Shh!" Jo pushed Samantha back against the wall of the corridor. Then she put her finger to her lips as Eddy rounded the corner. She whispered to both of them. "Someone is in there, I heard voices."

Samantha peered at the label on the placard beside the door.

"It's the main security office. It must be a security guard." Samantha frowned as she watched the door. "If they catch us in the corridor, they're going to escort us back to our cabins."

"Maybe we can create a distraction?" Jo shrugged as she watched the door as well. She took a sharp breath as the door swung open a few inches. She braced herself, expecting to be caught. But a second later she realized it had just shifted due to the movement of the ship. The opening allowed the voices inside to be more audible.

"Listen, I get it. He was so much older than you. I know what it must have been like to have to pretend to be attracted to him. I'm not going to judge you for what happened here."

"That's Blake." Eddy narrowed his eyes.

"I don't know what you're talking about." A woman replied.

"I'm pretty sure that's Annabella." Samantha inched a little closer to the door.

"This doesn't have to be difficult. All I'm asking is that you give me a cut of the inheritance, and in exchange, I'll keep my mouth shut about all of this. Deal?"

A huge wave crashed over the side. The ship abruptly lurched and Samantha stumbled back into Eddy's arms, Jo slid along the wall and bumped into Samantha. The door to the security office slammed shut, and the lights in the corridor flickered, then cut off. Bathed in darkness, the three friends huddled close together.

"In here." Samantha pushed open a door in the corridor and tugged her two friends inside. It was a small supplies closet with barely enough room for them to squeeze into. She was relieved that this closet didn't have a lock. The lights flickered on in the corridor as the door to the closet closed.

"Get back to your cabin!" Blake shouted over the alarms that began to buzz throughout the ship. "Stay there. If we need to evacuate, I will come and get you." A door slammed shut. "I'm on my way!" He barked as he ran down the corridor. The sound of softer footsteps soon followed him.

"It's now or never to get to that room." Eddy cleared his throat. "Let's go, if we're going."

"We're going." Jo stepped forward. "Those two were in there plotting to let that kid take the fall for the murder of an innocent man. No one deserves that. We need to find out how she pulled this off before she gets away with it, and Todd is still the best way to do that."

Samantha took a deep breath as she followed after Jo and Eddy. She glanced over her shoulder in the direction that Blake and Annabella had gone. She wanted to chase after them and demand an explanation, but she knew that wouldn't benefit anyone. All either of them had to do was deny what was said. She had no evidence to prove that they were involved in Carson's death. But maybe Todd would. Maybe he had overheard something, or witnessed something, that would prove Annabella's connection to the murder. It still didn't explain why Todd was following them, though.

Jo easily picked the lock, then pushed open the door. Once everyone was inside, she pushed the door closed behind them.

"I have no idea how long we have. Another security guard could come along at any second." Jo frowned as she rounded the desk and began to type on the computer. "It's not like there's a window to use for an escape." She glanced up at the four solid walls, then sighed as she looked back at the computer. "It has a password."

"Here, let me try." Samantha took over the keyboard. She typed in the most common passwords. When all were rejected, her stomach churned. Had they come all this way just to be blocked out of the system?

"Ladies." Eddy held up a folder and smiled. "Technology is not always the answer. There's a copy of the passenger manifest in here." He flipped the folder open.

Jo pulled out her phone and snapped a picture of the list.

"Hurry, put it back where you found it and let's get out of here before someone comes back." Jo looked up towards the closed door.

Samantha had never known Jo to be so nervous. Normally her confidence was off the charts. Perhaps it was the combination of the storm and the tiny office that left her frazzled. It certainly left Samantha frazzled. She cracked open the door and peeked out.

"The corridor is still clear."

"Great, let's go." Jo glanced at Eddy. "Is

everything back in place?"

"I think so." Eddy joined them at the door.

Samantha peeked out again. She didn't see anyone coming in either direction. She took a deep breath, then stepped out into the corridor.

"What are you doing?" The question sent ice through Samantha's veins as she quickly closed the door behind her before Eddy or Jo could step out.

Samantha's heart pounded against her chest as she stared into the eyes of a person she thought was a murderer.

"I was looking for you." She cleared her throat.

"Me?" Annabella crossed her arms as she stared back at Samantha. "In the security office?"

"Well, I was looking for you first. I went to your cabin to check on you, to make sure that you were okay in this storm. But you weren't there, even though everyone was supposed to be in their cabins. I got worried. So, I came here looking for Blake to see if he knew where you were." Samantha glanced over her shoulder at the office. "He wasn't in there, though. I guess he's busy with the storm."

"I'm sure he is." Annabella raised an eyebrow. "Why would you want to check on me?"

"I know that things didn't end well between us." Samantha sighed and clasped her hands together.

"But as the storm started to get worse, all I could think of was you all alone, after just losing your husband, and I just couldn't stand it. I had to know that you were okay."

"Really?" Annabella chuckled, then shook her head. "All of a sudden you're a fan of mine?"

"I'm sorry, I never meant to upset you. I used to report on crimes for a living, I was a crime journalist. I guess some of my old tactics came to the surface. I'm really sorry for that." Samantha stepped closer to Annabella and hoped that the woman wouldn't attempt to go into the security office.

"I see." Annabella pursed her lips, then exhaled. "I guess that gives you the right to be horrible. It's not like I don't expect it. Of course, everyone suspects me."

"I'm very sorry, Annabella." Samantha gulped as wind roared past the ship. "We should really get somewhere safe. Do you hear that wind?"

"I do." Annabella glanced at the ceiling as the ship trembled. "It's a little terrifying."

"I'll walk with you back to your cabin. It's on the way to mine." The wind howled. "Let's go, before it gets worse."

"Hopefully, it'll pass quickly." Annabella's eyes widened, then filled with tears. "Carson would know what to do. He had so much life experience. That's what fascinated me about him in the first place. He knew so much, had lived in so many places and met so many people." Her voice shivered as she took a breath. "I have no idea what to do now that he's gone."

Samantha gritted her teeth. After overhearing Annabella's conversation with Blake, it was hard not to be disgusted by the woman's attempt to solicit sympathy.

"Don't worry, Annabella, we're in good hands with the crew on this ship. I'm sure they've been through many storms like this before." Samantha steered her down the corridor away from the security office. Sparing only a brief glance over her shoulder, she hoped that Eddy and Jo would be able to get out before any security guards returned.

"I'm not so sure how much I trust the people on this ship. Did you hear that Nick has been detained?" Annabella wiped at her eyes. "I can't believe it. He was so kind to Carson and me. Why would he want to hurt him?"

"I'm not sure." Samantha looked at her for a moment. "Did you ever notice anyone else following you, Annabella? I know Nick was always around, but was there someone else that often seemed to be where you were? Someone following you?"

"Just the writer, James." Annabella shrugged.

"Do you know Todd Carpenter?"

"Who?" Annabella frowned. "No."

"Was anyone else following you?" Samantha asked.

"I don't know, the hotel and the ship were so crowded, I could barely keep track of Carson." Annabella squeezed her eyes shut as they reached her cabin. "All I keep thinking is that I never should have left Carson alone. All I had to do was stay with him. If I had, none of this would have happened. I just wanted a few drinks, to relax, after all of the craziness of the wedding. I knew that when Carson's nephews found out about us being married, they were going to be furious. I just needed a little time to think."

"Were Carson and his nephews close?"

"Those three fools only came around when they thought Carson might be on death's door. They didn't send him birthday cards, or even call him at Christmas. But if he was in the hospital, or had to have a medical procedure done, they hounded me for updates and information." Annabella looked back at Samantha. "At first, I thought it was sweet, caring of them to be so involved in their uncle's life, until I realized that they were just hoping for the worst. They wanted him dead. It was very clear to me. But Carson, all he saw was them taking the time out of their young, busy lives, to check on their old uncle. He was completely enamored with them. He always wanted me to keep tabs on their lives and try to stay in touch, so I did. I didn't have the heart to point out the truth to him. It would have crushed him."

"I'm sorry to hear that." Samantha sighed. "It's hard to believe that anyone could be so cruel."

"It is. I just needed time to think about things. Then there was Karl. He was so charming. He flirted with me, and I decided to go with it to take my mind off things. I won't ever forgive myself for flirting with another man while my husband was being murdered. I mean, how can I?" Annabella leaned against the door of her cabin as tears flowed down her cheeks. "I really am a terrible person."

Samantha couldn't resist. She put her arms around Annabella. She certainly was a good liar, and despite Samantha's certainty that she was involved with her husband's death, she couldn't fight the urge to comfort the woman. Maybe she really did regret Carson being dead, maybe she had loved him after all. Samantha pulled away, determined not to be sucked into Annabella's manipulation.

"You should go inside. I need to check on my friends and make sure that they are okay. When I find them, I will come back to make sure that you're safe. Okay?" Samantha did her best to sound genuine.

"Sure, thank you." Annabella clutched at the collar of her shirt, then stepped into the cabin.

Samantha heard the lock engage. She frowned as she looked down the corridor. She didn't dare to call Eddy or Jo on their phones, as if they were still hiding, the phone ringing might draw attention to them. However, she also didn't want to be out in the corridor for a security guard to spot. Without the picture of the list to guide her, she had no idea where Todd's cabin was. Frustrated, she decided to retrace her steps. Before she got very far, she received a text from Jo with a picture.

We are headed to his cabin.

Samantha sighed with relief, then sent a text in return.

I will meet you there.

Samantha enlarged the photograph until she could see Todd's cabin number. It was two floors down. She headed for the steps as quickly as she could. The ship went from rocking now and then to reminding her of bad turbulence on an airplane. She heard a few screams from the inside of cabins along her route. If she wasn't so focused on finding Todd, she probably would have been just as frightened. When she reached the fourth deck, she spotted Eddy and Jo about midway down the corridor.

"Hey!" Samantha hissed and waved her hand in the air to get their attention.

Jo jumped, then turned. She smiled as she caught sight of Samantha.

"Eddy, wait." Jo placed her hand on Eddy's arm just as Eddy steadied himself on the wall of the corridor.

"Can you believe this?" Eddy looked at Samantha, his eyes wide, and his skin pale. She guessed that he might be getting a little seasick from all of the rocking.

"This is probably the worst of it." Samantha bit down into her bottom lip. "At least, I hope it is."

"Me too." Jo tipped her head towards a cabin a few doors down. "That's the one. Are we ready for this?"

"He should be in there." Samantha marched

forward, the best she could, as the floor shifted and jerked beneath her.

"Last time I spoke to Walt he said it was going to be pretty fierce." Jo took a deep breath. "Let's hope this is one of those times when he is actually wrong."

"Not much chance of that." Eddy grimaced, then followed after Samantha.

CHAPTER 16

Samantha paused in front of the door of the cabin that belonged to Todd. She gave it a swift and solid pound, though she had no idea what she would say to Todd once he opened the door. Several seconds passed with no response.

"Maybe he's not in there?" Jo pursed her lips.

"He should be. Everyone is supposed to be in their cabins." Eddy nodded to Samantha. "Knock again, harder this time."

"Okay." Samantha swung her fist against the door as hard as she could, several times.

The door to the cabin next to Todd's swung open. A woman peered at the three people in the corridor.

"What's all the racket? Is there an evacuation

order?" The woman braced herself against the door frame as the ship shifted.

"Connie?" Samantha met her eyes. "Is Karl in there with you?"

"I'm right here." Karl glared out at the three of them. "What are you three doing out of your cabins?"

"We were looking for your neighbor Todd." Eddy pointed to the still closed door. "Have you seen him?"

"No, we haven't." Karl guided Connie back into the cabin. "Unlike you, we know how to mind our own business." He pushed the door shut, hard.

Samantha frowned. "I don't think that Todd is in there."

"Where else would he be?" Eddy glanced down the corridor. "In weather like this I would think most people would stay inside."

"Unless they have a reason not to be." Samantha narrowed her eyes. "Maybe he's out looking for Annabella."

"Or maybe he's in there and just doesn't want to answer." Jo reached into her pocket. "I can check."

"No, don't." Samantha frowned as the lights in the corridor flickered. "Things are too chaotic to risk getting caught breaking in. I'm sure if he was in there he would have responded." She glanced back in the direction of Karl's room. "If his cabin is right next to Todd's, Todd really might have seen something. He could even be out looking for someone to report the information to. We just have to stay focused on finding him." She pressed her hand against her stomach as the ship rocked hard. She did her best to steady her stomach. It wouldn't do to get sick in the middle of an investigation. "Jo, can you get through to Walt?"

"I've been trying, nothing is going through." Jo frowned. "I'm sure he's worried about us. Wait, let me try Blake." She pulled her phone from her pocket. "He would want to know that a passenger wasn't in his cabin. I can tell him that Todd is missing, and he will have everyone on the ship searching for him."

"That's the best thing we can do right now." Samantha looked up and down the corridor. "If he's somewhere outside of a cabin, then he'll be spotted quickly by the security guards."

"It's worth a shot." Eddy nodded, then braced himself against the wall. "You make the call, I'm going up on deck to see if I can spot anyone. He could be in trouble."

"Not by yourself you're not." Samantha grabbed his hand. "I'm going with you."

"Sam, it's not safe up there." Eddy met her eyes. "It's too risky."

"We'll all go." Jo ended the call. "Blake said he will have the security guards looking for Todd. But now he also knows that we are not in our cabins. I assured him that we are going back there right now, so we'll have to watch out for the guards, too."

"Last chance to find Todd." Eddy mounted the stairs that led up to the deck. "Everyone with me?"

"Right behind you." Samantha called out.

"Just make sure you stay upright." Jo half-chuckled, while the wind howled down the stairs at them. "Wow, maybe this wasn't such a good idea."

"We'll just have a look." Samantha gripped the railing on the stairs tight and pulled herself up them, despite the force of the wind. Once on the deck, she could barely see from the rain that rushed past her. Waves crashed over the railing of the ship, flooding the deck. The water was still raging from the storm.

Eddy reached back and grabbed her hand. He pulled her in front of him. Then he did the same for Jo.

"You two stay ahead of me so I can see where you are."

Samantha gestured for Jo to take the lead.

They made their way along the deck. A loud, sharp sound cut through the roar of the wind. It sent a shiver down Eddy's spine.

"That was a gunshot!" Eddy looked over his shoulder and saw a figure not far behind them. "Someone is shooting at us! Run!"

Samantha did her best to obey his command, but the wind fought against her. The rain began to subside, and the wind finally began to die down.

"Go faster!" Eddy placed his hand on the small of Samantha's back and gave her a light shove.

"I'm going as fast as I can!" Samantha scowled over her shoulder at him, then tried to push her legs faster. Jo remained only a few steps ahead of her.

"Eddy, we're running out of deck!" Jo gasped as she realized there were no nearby doors or stairways to take cover in. A long wall ran along one side of them, and the railing ran along the other side.

"Keep going." Eddy gulped down a breath as he heard the footsteps behind him quicken. "I think whoever it is knows that we're trapped. We'll have to think of something."

"There's nowhere to go." Jo reached the railing,

then peered over the top rung. "There are lifeboats down here, that's it."

"Can you get to them?" Eddy and Samantha reached the railing as well.

"We'll have to jump a bit of distance, but yes, I think we can get in." Jo shot a quick look over her shoulder, then met Samantha's eyes. "It's our only choice. We're not going to get out of this any other way."

"If we stay in the lifeboat, we'll be sitting ducks!" Samantha frowned.

"I can get us to safety once we're in the boat, I know I can. The storm and water have died down." Jo held her hand out to her. "Sam, we have to go!"

"Yes, go!" Eddy nodded as he looked over his shoulder as well. "Hurry, we don't have much time!"

"I'll go first, Sam, that way I can guide you!" Jo pulled herself up over the railing and leaped from the top rung.

"Jo!" Samantha shrieked as she watched her friend sail through the air, then land on both feet squarely in the center of one of the lifeboats attached to the side of the ship. The boat rocked slightly but remained attached to the rope that held it in place.

"You can do it, Sam!" Jo waved to her. "Just get

your leg over the top railing and I'll make sure you land in the right place!"

Samantha's heart pounded. She had never been more certain that she couldn't do something. But she knew that Jo and Eddy's lives hung in the balance. If she hesitated much longer, they would likely all be caught. With her heart still in her throat she climbed over the top railing. It was slick and cold from the rain that still fell in intermittent spurts from the dark sky. Her stomach churned as she looked over the edge of the ship towards the lifeboat below. Jo waved to her again.

"I'm here, just jump, Sam, I'll make sure you get into the boat." Jo's heart slammed against her chest as she looked up at her friend. She knew it would be a huge risk for Samantha to take, she just hoped that she would trust her enough to take it.

Samantha took a deep breath then launched herself over the railing. She closed her eyes tight as she fell through the air. When her feet struck something solid, she felt warm, strong arms wrap around her to steady her.

"You did it, you're safe." Jo met her eyes as Samantha opened them. Then she looked back up at the ship. "Eddy, let's go!"

Eddy peered over the railing. He heard the

heavy steps of someone not far behind him. He realized that there wouldn't be time to jump into the boat and pull the lever to release the lifeboat into the water. If he jumped in, they would all be stuck there, waiting for whoever chased them to attack. He grabbed the lever.

"Eddy, what are you doing?" Samantha shouted as the wind picked up. "Eddy!"

"Be careful on the water!" Eddy shouted back and pulled the lever. The lifeboat lurched, then slid swiftly down towards the water.

"Eddy, no!" Samantha shrieked. But she already knew it was too late. In the same moment that the boat hit the water with a hard splash, the sound of a gunshot cut through the rumble of distant thunder and the howl of the wind.

CHAPTER 17

The sound of the gunshot echoed through Samantha's ears. She couldn't make a sound for several seconds after she heard it. When she finally found her voice, she looked over at Jo.

"Did you hear that?" Samantha clutched at her chest as Jo struggled to start the motor. After a couple more tries, she gave up and picked up the oars.

"Sam, you have to sit down!" Jo winced as spray off the large waves struck her in the face. "Sit down!"

Samantha sunk down into the boat. Tears filled her eyes.

"Do you think he was shot, Jo?" She looked across the boat at her friend.

"No, I don't think so." Jo narrowed her eyes. "I won't think it. We don't know anything for sure. We just have to do what he told us to and be careful in the water. Hopefully, now that the storm has died down the coastguard will be here soon, and they will find us, but we have to make sure we keep the boat afloat until then."

"Yes, yes, you're right." Samantha tried to sound brave, but tears slipped down her cheeks. What if he was shot? What if he was gone forever? Her stomach twisted with a mixture of fear and grief. She wanted to believe, as Jo did, that everything was fine. But without Eddy at her side, she realized, that nothing was fine.

"Samantha!" Jo barked at her as the wind continued to die down. "Listen to me. We can't do anything to help Eddy if we don't stay afloat. You have to help me. I can't start the motor, we have to use the oars."

"Okay, yes." Samantha forced herself to focus on the matter at hand. She positioned herself better in the boat and took one of the oars from Jo. Between the two of them they managed to steady the boat in the water, despite the rolling waves that were stirred up by the remnants of the storm. "I think it's finally coming to an end." She looked up at the sky, where a bit of sunlight peeked through the thick clouds.

"We can hope so." Jo frowned as she looked over the sky as well. "Let's just hope there isn't another storm coming. We need to stay close to the ship. Otherwise it might be hard for anyone to find us."

"I'm trying." Samantha dug the paddle through the water. "But the current is taking us away from it."

"I know." Jo frowned as she did her best to navigate the boat as well. The sirens that were blaring on the ship ceased.

"It sounds like the emergency signal has been called off." Samantha's stomach twisted as she wondered if they'd found Eddy yet. "Maybe we can get closer." She paddled harder.

"No, Samantha, stop. You're just going to exhaust yourself." Jo frowned as she watched the ship grow more distant. "We're not strong enough to battle the current. We're better off just focusing on navigating these waves."

"But if we get too far—"

"I know." Jo closed her eyes for just a moment, then took a breath. "We will be fine, Sam, I promise. But we have to keep afloat."

"Right." Samantha gazed at the ship a moment longer, then turned her attention to using the paddle to steady them as they went over the large waves that still rolled beneath them.

On the ship, Eddy shuddered as he held his hands in the air. The person before him continued to train the gun on him.

"Who else knows?"

"No one." Eddy swallowed hard as he stared at the man before him. "No one else, just me."

"Don't lie to me." He moved closer to Eddy, his finger on the trigger. "Those first shots were a warning, the next one won't be."

"I'm the only one. I was trying to get away from you." Eddy lowered his hands just enough to ease the burning in his shoulders. After the second gunshot he'd run, but he hadn't gotten far before the man tackled him. Now, held at gunpoint, Eddy was certain that his life would soon be over. The only thing he could do, was attempt to protect his friends. "Todd, it doesn't have to end like this. I know you weren't working alone."

"You do?" Todd eyed Eddy over the top of the

gun. "It doesn't matter though, does it? I'm the one that got my hands dirty."

"It does matter." Eddy's heart began to pound as he sensed a crack in the man's resolve. "Especially if you cooperate with the police. All you have to do is turn Annabella in, and the police will go easy on you."

"Annabella?" Todd blinked, then smiled. "Oh, you actually don't have a clue, do you?" He ran his free hand through his hair. "You know, I told myself it would be worth it. I would just have to do something to someone who would die soon anyway. Then I would be rich. I would even get to enjoy the cruise. I used to work on cruise ships, but this would actually be the first vacation I've ever been on."

Eddy's thoughts spun as he wondered who Todd was working with. If it wasn't Annabella, then who? Or was he just trying to protect her still?

"I understand the feeling. This is my first cruise. When I was your age, I never once took a vacation." Eddy cleared his throat. "You have to work hard to get by in this world."

"Too hard." Todd clenched his jaw, then shook his head. "Not everyone can do it, you know. Some of us, we have to try so much harder than other people. So, when I was offered the chance to make more money than I could in the next ten years of my life, just for doing an old friend a favor, how could I possibly turn that down?"

"You couldn't." Eddy squinted at him. The rain had died down to a light drizzle, but it was still enough to hamper his view. Yes, the barrel of that gun was still pointed at him. He cringed and lowered his eyes. "No jury would expect you to be able to turn an offer like that down. Right now, you have one body on your hands, Todd. Not to be cold, but how many years did he really have left? He was old. Me on the other hand, I still have time, Todd. A jury isn't going to care much about a man who had one foot in the grave, but they are going to care if you kill someone who still had time left. You've got a decision to make here."

"You don't look like you've got that much time left." Todd quirked an eyebrow and offered a cruel smile. "You have one foot in the grave too, don't you, old timer?"

"No, I don't." Eddy narrowed his eyes. "Both of my feet are firmly planted, right here, in front of you."

"I'm sorry, but you're the only one who knows about what really happened on this ship. As it stands, some kid is going to end up in prison for what I did, and maybe even that old man's girlfriend." Todd shrugged. "The only person that stands between me and freedom, is you."

"Wait!" Eddy's eyes widened as he realized that Todd was not aware of some very important information. "Don't you mean wife?"

"Excuse me?" He lowered the gun just an inch or two.

"That's right. Annabella and Carson were married. He didn't have a will, so she is going to get everything." Eddy nodded. "Isn't that why she got you to kill him?"

"What? They were married? You have no idea what you're talking about." Todd looked confused.

"Did Nick help you do it?" Eddy asked.

"Nick? No, he's just going to take the fall for it." Todd took a step forward.

"Were you working with the guy taking the photos, the writer, James?" Eddy asked, but he really didn't believe that James would have pointed Jo in Todd's direction if they were both involved in the murder.

"James?" Todd waved the gun. "What are you talking about? Have you lost your mind, old man?"

Maybe it wasn't Annabella, Nick or James.

Eddy searched his mind to come up with an answer to the question that plagued him. If it wasn't Annabella, Nick, or James that hired or helped Todd, who was left? Bobby? "I guess Bobby really had a bone to pick with Carson. How much did he pay you?"

"Bobby?" Todd blinked, then raised the gun again. "I have no idea who you're talking about. Did Carson really get married? Annabella's going to get everything?"

All at once it clicked in Eddy's mind. He knew exactly who had hired Todd to kill Carson.

"Oh Todd." Eddy frowned as he lowered his hands. "You have no idea what you've done."

"I know exactly what I've done." Todd tapped his finger lightly against the trigger. "Now, it's time to get rid of you." As he spoke, the sirens on the ship suddenly cut off.

"What now?" Eddy stared at him. "The wind has died down. If you shoot me now, people are going to hear the gunshot. There are security guards all over the place. Do you really think you'll be able to get away before they find you?"

CHAPTER 18

Walt frowned as Jo's voicemail picked up for what felt like the hundredth time. Ever since the latest weather update, he'd been trying to reach his friends on the ship, but none of his calls had gone through. As much as he wanted to believe that it was just bad reception, he grew more and more concerned with each minute that passed. He looked up the cruise line's phone number, and dialed it. After several minutes of waiting, a strained voice picked up.

"Chorus Cruises. How can I help you?"

"I'm trying to check on the well-being of a few of my friends on board one of your ships. The Chorus of the Ocean."

"Ah yes, we've had quite a few calls about that

particular ship. Unfortunately, there have been a few incidents that sent it off its planned course, and so it is facing some inclement weather at the moment. But all the reports from the captain have been that everyone on the ship is safe, and that they will soon be clear of the storm. There is no reason to be concerned."

"Are you certain?" Walt frowned. "I've been trying to reach my friends, and none of my calls seem to be going through."

"It's possible that they are in an area of the ocean where cell service is spotty at best. Give it an hour or two and I'm sure that you will be able to reach them. I'm afraid that's all I can do for you right now, sir." Her tone brightened. "I'm sure that your friends are having a wonderful time."

"Thanks." Walt ended the call with his heart in his throat. No matter what the cheerful voice on the phone claimed, his gut told him that something was off. He'd been able to reach them not long before, and now he couldn't reach them at all. Yes, it was possible that the ship had drifted into a dead zone, but he doubted it. He just knew there was something wrong. He tried Eddy's cell phone again. It rang, then cut off and went to his voicemail. He frowned as he hung up the phone.

He began to pace back and forth through the hotel room. What if something happened to them and they had no idea how to reach him, or to otherwise call for help? What if him staying behind in the hotel was the reason that his friends were in trouble now?

"Not now, Walt, this is not the time to lose it." Walt picked up his phone again. He called Eddy's contact at the police department near Sage Gardens. He knew that if anyone could help him, it would be Chris. However, he'd never even spoken to Chris before. He had no idea if Chris would be willing to help. After the first ring, he picked up.

"Hi Chris, this is Walt. Walter Right, I'm a friend of Eddy's."

"I know who you are, Walt."

"You do?" Walt's eyes widened.

"Yes, Eddy has talked about you plenty. Is everything okay?"

"Actually, it's not." Walt sighed, relieved by Chris' friendly tone. "I might be overreacting, but I have a feeling that Eddy, Jo, and Samantha are in a lot of trouble on their cruise. I am staying at the hotel by the dock until they get back. Did you know that Eddy was going on a cruise?"

"Yes, Eddy told me before he left. He also asked

me to look into something while he was on the ship. What has you concerned?"

"There's a bad storm, and they're in the middle of it. I haven't been able to reach any of them, and the cruise company won't do anything to help me." Walt frowned. "You'll probably think I'm crazy for being so worried."

"Not at all. Eddy has always told me, if Walt thinks something is off, you'd better believe him." Chris paused. "I just looked up the storm, and I can see that it's pretty fierce, but the worst of it is out of the area now."

"I saw that, too, but I still can't reach them. Maybe the ship isn't in an area with cell service? Maybe cell service is down?"

"I can check that. Just a second." Chris paused, then cleared his throat. "No, there are no reported outages in the area. I'll tell you what, let me see who I can get hold of to find out some information."

"There might be something that could help." Walt lowered his voice. "Jo is a dear friend of mine, but she has a tendency to go off on her own and get into some risky situations. The last time she did this, I might have uh, installed a locator on her phone."

"Clever." Chris chuckled. "Yes, I know all about Jo, too. Why don't you see if you can pinpoint a location and I'll update you as soon as I've spoken with a few people."

"Thanks Chris." Walt began to feel calmer as he hung up the phone. He turned on the tracking application on his phone. Now that he knew there was service in the area, he hoped that the tracker would work. A few seconds later the location of Jo's phone popped up. But it didn't make him calmer, not at all. It was in the middle of the ocean, which was to be expected, since she was on a cruise ship. However, the location of the cruise ship, which he had open on his computer, was about three miles away.

"Jo!" Walt stood up from his chair. "Just what are you doing out there?"

His phone rang before he had a chance to dial Chris' number again.

"Hello?"

"It's Chris. I was able to get a hold of the head security guard on the ship. He said that they are not in their cabins, and they are investigating a missing lifeboat." Chris paused. "Did you know there was a murder on the ship?"

"Yes." Walt sighed and closed his eyes. "And I think I know where that missing lifeboat is. I'm going to send you the coordinates." He typed a text out to Chris, then hit send. He put the phone back to his ear. "Did you get it?"

"Yes, I'll forward the information. Walt, someone from the local police department is going to meet you in the lobby of the hotel. I'm sorry, I wish I could do more, but this is the most I can offer." Chris sighed. "I'm sure they'll be fine."

"Thanks Chris. You did more than I could. I really appreciate your help. I'm sure they will be fine, too." Walt hung up the phone, without an ounce of certainty that his friends were safe. Why would they be out on a lifeboat? Was it all of them? Just Jo? Just her phone? His heart raced as he began to panic. How could he possibly help them when he was stuck on land? He grabbed his phone, and his computer, and headed down to the lobby to meet the local police.

CHAPTER 19

Samantha shivered as she shifted on the seat in the boat. The ship was now just a dot in the distance.

"Jo, we should rest if we can." She looked over at her friend, who continued to plunge her paddle into the water that was finally calm.

"You're right." Jo rested her paddle on the side of the boat. She bit into her bottom lip.

"It's all right, you can say it." Samantha stretched her arms out. Her shoulders were sore from paddling, and in general she was exhausted.

"Say what?" Jo met her eyes.

"We're not going to be easy to be found now, are we?" Samantha shook her head as she looked up at the darkening sky. "It's going to be too dark now for them to even look for us. I doubt anyone even knows we're missing."

"Eddy does." Jo reached across the boat and patted Samantha's knee. "I'm sure he's already gotten help."

"You mean if he wasn't shot?" Samantha winced at the words. "I'm sorry, I shouldn't have said that. I shouldn't even think it."

"It's okay, Sam, you don't have to apologize to me." Jo took a deep breath, then let it out through her lips slowly. "You're not wrong. We have no idea what happened to Eddy. I want to believe that he's okay. But we don't know that. It is possible that no one knows we're missing."

"Maybe we should try our phones again. Maybe there's service now that the storm has passed." Samantha reached into her pocket for her phone. When she pulled it out, she found that it was soaked. "Oh no, it must have gotten wet in the storm, or I must have splashed it when I was paddling. I don't think it's going to work now. What about yours?"

"I haven't even thought about it." Jo touched her back pocket. "It's still here, it feels dry." Jo pulled her phone out, then frowned. "But the battery is almost dead. I could probably only get one call out of it. If anyone puts me on hold or if it rings out or goes to voicemail, we're going to be out of luck."

"Who should we call? There's not much chance that Eddy still has his phone, and if he does, I doubt it has battery." Samantha frowned.

"Walt. I'll call Walt." Jo's eyes lit up. "If he knows we're in trouble he'll do anything to get us to safety."

"Good idea." Samantha smiled. "Hurry before—"

"It's too late." Jo sighed as she stared at her phone. "As soon as I selected dial, it shut down. I'm sorry, Sam. I should have thought about it sooner."

"Don't be sorry, Jo." Samantha forced down a sob that threatened to escape. "We just have to stay positive."

"What did you say?" Jo leaned forward as a loud sound drowned out her friend's voice. "What is that sound?" She craned her neck and looked up at the sky.

"It's a helicopter!" Samantha gasped. Without a second thought she whipped off her jacket and began to wave it in the air.

"Samantha!" Jo stared at her. "What are you doing? It's so cold."

"We have to get their attention, Jo or they'll fly right past!" Samantha continued to wave her jacket.

Jo winced, but removed her jacket, and began to wave it as well. The helicopter swirled the water around them as it hovered above them.

"We're coming down to get you!" The voice echoed through the air, strengthened by the bullhorn that projected it. "Stay put!"

Samantha shrieked with happiness as she tugged her jacket back on. Jo laughed as she zipped hers up.

"How did they find us?" Jo shook her head.

"I don't care, I just can't wait to get off this boat!" Samantha watched as a man in a bright yellow vest was lowered down towards their boat. She'd never been so relieved to see another human being before.

Minutes later, they were both in the helicopter, headed back to land.

"Please, you have to help us. I think our friend might have been shot." Samantha filled in one of her rescuers on the situation that they faced just before they ended up in the lifeboat.

"That's some story." The man gazed at her. "Don't worry, we already have police on board the cruise ship. I'll make sure they conduct a search for your friend."

"Wait, if Eddy didn't tell you to look for us, then who did?" Jo met the man's eyes.

"Someone was keeping a close eye on you." He winked at her as the helicopter landed. As soon as the blades slowed, a man emerged from a waiting police car. He rushed towards the helicopter. As Jo stepped out of the helicopter, she recognized him right away.

"Walt!" Jo gasped as she flung her arms around him. "What are you doing here?"

"No time for that." Samantha gave them a forceful shove towards the police car. "We need to find Eddy!"

On the drive to the dock, Walt filled them in on how he hunted them down in the water. He braced himself as he looked at Jo.

"Please, don't be angry at me."

"How can I be?" Jo laughed as she squeezed his hand. "You saved my life, Walt. We'll have a little talk about boundaries once we make sure Eddy is safe and sound."

As they pulled up to the dock, it was impossible to miss the massive ship that waited for them.

Samantha ran towards the ship, as her heart

raced. She knew that within seconds she would know the truth about Eddy. She almost wanted to slow down. If Eddy wasn't okay, she didn't want to find out. As she reached the top of the ramp, she spotted a man in handcuffs.

"Todd?" Samantha blinked as she recognized the man from the picture.

Jo started up the ramp as well, but hesitated when she glanced at Walt.

"You can stay here if you want."

"No." Walt took her hand and held it tight. "Wherever you go, I'm going, too." He held his breath as he led the way up the ramp onto the ship.

"Blake!" Samantha shouted as she saw him being led away by an officer. "Where is Eddy?"

"I'm right here." Eddy stepped out from behind a paramedic that had been looking him over. "Samantha, Jo!" He smiled wider than Samantha had ever seen him smile. "I'm so glad you're safe!"

Samantha launched herself into his arms. She didn't think about the deck still being slippery from the rain. As Eddy stumbled back, he lost his footing, and he ended up flat on his back, with Samantha sprawled across him.

"Wait! Come back!" Eddy laughed as he waved

at the paramedic. "On second thought, I'm sure I'll be just fine."

Samantha's cheeks burned as she managed to get to her feet.

"I'm sorry, Eddy, I was so worried about you. I heard a gunshot, I thought—"

"Don't worry anymore." Eddy looked into her eyes. "I'm fine, Sam, I'm right here, and I'm fine."

"Thank goodness you are." Walt shook his head. "I knew cruises could be dangerous, but this, this really takes the cake."

"I don't understand." Samantha glanced over her shoulder. "Why did they arrest Todd?"

"Todd was the one chasing us. He intended to shoot me, but he didn't get the chance." Eddy tipped his head towards Todd's black eye. "I managed to talk some sense into him. Actually, I distracted him. Carson's nephew, Caleb, is the one who hired him. Caleb and Todd are friends from school. He told Todd that he needed him to kill his uncle before he had the chance to marry Annabella. He had arranged to work in the area near the hotel for a few days so he could arrange Carson's murder with Todd. He knew once Carson married Annabella, he would lose his inheritance. Apparently, his finances took a hard hit when he switched jobs. It was the perfect alibi as he wasn't even on the ship. Little did Caleb know that Carson already married Annabella." He watched as Todd was led down the ramp.

"Quite an elaborate scheme." Jo mused.

"And here comes Karl." Eddy watched as Karl was escorted out onto the deck by another police officer. "Karl and Todd used to work together. They are both strapped for cash. Caleb hired Karl to help him. He and his wife got a free cruise out of it. He got Karl to distract Annabella and keep her away from Carson. Todd then dressed up as Carson and went back to his cabin. He thought it would buy them more time and make it look like Annabella had something to do with the murder. Caleb had to make sure that the body was found at some point so Carson would be declared deceased, otherwise no one could access his money. He's a pretty smart guy for being a complete idiot." Eddy frowned.

"Did Nick help them as well?" Samantha asked.

"No, Nick will be released, he had nothing to do with any of it. Karl planted the clothes in Nick's cabin. Blake on the other hand, he is going to face some charges, because Annabella turned him in." Eddy shrugged.

"That's right." Jo narrowed her eyes. "What

kind of explanation did she have for that conversation?"

"Apparently, it was more one-sided than we realized. Blake assumed that Annabella had hired Nick to kill Carson and offered to keep her secret for a share of the money. Of course, as it turns out Annabella had nothing to do with it. The real murderer, the one that orchestrated it, wasn't even on the ship." Eddy crossed his arms. "He's being taken into custody as well."

Samantha watched as Annabella stood beside another police officer. She spoke quietly to him.

"To think all this time we suspected her, and she really was grieving her husband, perhaps the love of her life."

"At least she knows the truth now. It's the best we can offer her." Eddy smiled slightly.

"Excuse me, I'm Sharon, with Chorus Cruises." A woman walked up to them with a bright smile. "I'd like to offer you a free cruise for all the trouble you experienced on this one."

"No thanks." Jo took a step back.

"Not a chance." Samantha shook her head.

"I'm never getting on a ship again." Eddy squinted at her. "But thanks for the offer."

"Now, now. It's important to confront and

overcome your fears." Walt grinned as he led his friends down off the ship.

"Oh, just get it over with, Walt." Eddy rolled his eyes.

"Get what over with?" Walt looked over at him.

"The 'I told you so's.'" Eddy grinned.

"No." Walt took a deep breath as he looked at his friends. "All I want to say is I'm happy we're all on solid ground, together."

"I can't wait to get home." Jo wrapped her arm around his waist and smiled at him. "We have a lot to talk about, Walt, don't we? Like downloading applications on other people's phones?"

"Let's not forget about the heroic rescue that it led to." Walt's eyes widened.

Samantha looped her arm through Eddy's. She smiled to herself as he pulled her closer to him. Maybe the rest of the world was beautiful, but she had no doubt in her mind that she had everything she needed right at home in Sage Gardens.

The End

ALSO BY CINDY BELL

SAGE GARDENS COZY MYSTERIES

Sage Gardens Cozy Mystery Series Box Set Volume 1 (Books 1 - 4)

Birthdays Can Be Deadly

Money Can Be Deadly

Trust Can Be Deadly

Ties Can Be Deadly

Rocks Can Be Deadly

Jewelry Can Be Deadly

Numbers Can Be Deadly

Memories Can Be Deadly

Paintings Can Be Deadly

Snow Can Be Deadly

Tea Can Be Deadly

Greed Can Be Deadly

Clutter Can Be Deadly

CHOCOLATE CENTERED COZY MYSTERIES

The Sweet Smell of Murder

A Deadly Delicious Delivery

A Bitter Sweet Murder

A Treacherous Tasty Trail

Pastry and Peril

Trouble and Treats

Fudge Films and Felonies

Custom-Made Murder

Skydiving, Soufflés and Sabotage

Christmas Chocolates and Crimes

Hot Chocolate and Homicide

Chocolate Caramels and Conmen

Picnics, Pies and Lies

Devils Food Cake and Drama

Cinnamon and a Corspe

Cherries, Berries and a Body

Christmas Cookies and Criminals

WAGGING TAIL COZY MYSTERIES

Murder at Pawprint Creek (prequel)

Murder at Pooch Park

Murder at the Pet Boutique

A Merry Murder at St. Bernard Cabins

Murder at the Dog Training Academy

Murder at Corgi Country Club

A Merry Murder on Ruff Road

DUNE HOUSE COZY MYSTERIES

Seaside Secrets

Boats and Bad Guys

Treasured History

Hidden Hideaways

Dodgy Dealings

Suspects and Surprises

Ruffled Feathers

A Fishy Discovery

Danger in the Depths

Celebrities and Chaos

Pups, Pilots and Peril

Tides, Trails and Trouble

Racing and Robberies

Athletes and Alibis

Manuscripts and Deadly Motives

Pelicans, Pier and Poison

Sand, Sea and a Skeleton

NUTS ABOUT NUTS COZY MYSTERIES

A Tough Case to Crack

A Seed of Doubt

Roasted Peanuts and Peril

Chestnuts, Camping and Culprits

DONUT TRUCK COZY MYSTERIES

Deadly Deals and Donuts

Fatal Festive Donuts

Bunny Donuts and a Body

Strawberry Donuts and Scandal

Frosted Donuts and Fatal Falls

BEKKI THE BEAUTICIAN COZY MYSTERIES

Hairspray and Homicide

A Dyed Blonde and a Dead Body

Mascara and Murder

Pageant and Poison

Conditioner and a Corpse

Mistletoe, Makeup and Murder

Hairpin, Hair Dryer and Homicide

Blush, a Bride and a Body

Shampoo and a Stiff

Cosmetics, a Cruise and a Killer

Lipstick, a Long Iron and Lifeless

Camping, Concealer and Criminals

Treated and Dyed

A Wrinkle-Free Murder

A MACARON PATISSERIE COZY MYSTERY SERIES

Sifting for Suspects

Recipes and Revenge

Mansions, Macarons and Murder

HEAVENLY HIGHLAND INN COZY MYSTERIES

Murdering the Roses

Dead in the Daisies

Killing the Carnations

Drowning the Daffodils

Suffocating the Sunflowers

Books, Bullets and Blooms

A Deadly Serious Gardening Contest

A Bridal Bouquet and a Body

Digging for Dirt

WENDY THE WEDDING PLANNER COZY MYSTERIES

Matrimony, Money and Murder

Chefs, Ceremonies and Crimes

Knives and Nuptials

Mice, Marriage and Murder

ABOUT THE AUTHOR

Cindy Bell is a USA Today and Wall Street Journal Bestselling Author. She is the author of the cozy mystery series Wagging Tail, Donut Truck, Dune House, Sage Gardens, Chocolate Centered, Macaron Patisserie, Nuts about Nuts, Bekki the Beautician, Heavenly Highland Inn and Wendy the Wedding Planner.

Cindy has always loved reading, but it is only recently that she has discovered her passion for writing romantic cozy mysteries. She loves walking along the beach thinking of the next adventure her characters can embark on.

You can sign up for her newsletter so you are notified of her latest releases at http://www.cindybellbooks.com.

Made in the USA
Coppell, TX
29 February 2020